L^{The}AND*O*^{of}PHIR

by Charles Beadle

Off-Trail Publications
Elkhorn, California

Front cover art by H.W. Wesso from
All Star Detective Stories, April 1930

THE LAND OF OPHIR
By Charles Beadle
Copyright © 2012, Off-Trail Publications
ISBN: 978-1-935031-19-2

OFF-TRAIL PUBLICATIONS
Elkhorn, California

Printed in the United States of America
First printing: March 2012

CONTENTS

— — *The Land of Ophir* — —
Serialized in ADVENTURE magazine

— — § — —

The World of Beadle
By John Locke

WE LAST VISITED CHARLES BEADLE for the 2007 Off-Trail collection, *The City of Baal*, which reprinted six of his stories from *Adventure*, and another from *The Frontier*. Beadle was a regular in *Adventure* from 1918-25. He also placed a number of tales in other American pulps.

In the *City of Baal* introduction, Beadle's biography was constructed primarily from his brief notes to *Adventure's* column, *The Camp-Fire*. We won't recount all the details, except to note that Beadle served in the British South African Police in Southern Rhodesia before the turn of the 20th Century, participated in the Boer war, afterwards traveled north through East Africa, and spent time in Morocco from 1908-12.

Henceforth, we'll fill in with new information that has surfaced. We'd especially like to thank Morgan Wallace, John Eggeling, Neil Pearson, and Patricia Wilkinson for advancing the research.

Beadle's date of birth and family background were mysteries in 2007, and can now be clarified. His father was Henry Beadle, a mariner born in the town of Barking (now a suburb of London), approximately 1844. In 1881, he was master of the British schooner *Cilurnum*, which included San Francisco and the Far East among its ports of call. He sailed with his wife Isabelle. Charles had two older brothers, Henry Jr. (*b.* ~1875) and William George (*b.* ~1876). The family address was in Hackney, just west of Barking. On October 27, 1881, Charles Beadle was born at sea, or, as he put it, "My native heath is somewhere in mid-Atlantic." In 1885, Isabelle died, and by the end of the year, Henry Beadle was remarried to Sarah Eleanor Killick (born in Liverpool, ~1844).

Patricia Wilkinson, Charles Beadle's great niece by way of William George, wrote to author Neil Pearson: "We thought [Charles] might have gone to Africa in search of his eldest brother Harry who disappeared in Rhodesia having gone out to Africa 'with Cecil Rhodes.' His father was a sea captain and came from a long line of sea captains. His wife travelled with him and died at sea [on the *Cilurnum*] from consumption when Charles was quite small. He had an odd upbringing."

Beadle wrote of his youth that he was "Educated at boarding-schools in England; hence no home life and consequent atrophy of the sentimentalities." He left home while still a teenager and began his travels and adventures.

He turned to writing during his Morocco years. His earliest known publication is an article in the October 1908 issue of *The Pall Mall Magazine*, "A Talk with the New Sultan of Morocco." It was illustrated with Beadle's photos and even included a photo of Beadle himself in desert robes. His first known fiction is the 1911 novel, *The City of Shadows: A Romance of Morocco*.

Beadle married Sylvia Grace Ellen Hornsby (*b*. 1891) in Paris sometime during 1911-15; she died in Cannes on September 13, 1915. Her considerable estate of £8,355 was left to Beadle and the artist Walter Edward Penn (who died in WWI). Beadle left Paris, sailed from Cádiz, Spain to New York City, arriving November 14, 1916, perhaps due to the turmoil of the Great War, or to escape bad memories. He established his pulp-writing career, took a trip to the West Coast (he was in San Francisco in September 1918), and by 1920 was back in Paris, submitting his stories from abroad.

His work didn't appear in *Adventure* after 1925; however, he made sporadic appearances in other pulps, notably *Short Stories*, while concentrating on writing novels directly for book publication. In *City of Baal*, we speculated that his five appearances in *Short Stories* during the '40s were reprints, and that he may have been deceased by then. Neither is the case. The last of the stories, "Nameless Spy" (June 10, 1947), is a contemporary tale set in French North Africa and refers to the Allied Forces. It's his last known published work, and the most recent evidence of his being alive. English records yield no clue as to his date of death, which probably indicates that he died in France. No doubt, there's a record there waiting to be discovered.

As for *The Land of Ophir*, it was Beadle's second serial for *Adventure* (after the four-part *Witch-Doctors* in 1919). *Witch-Doctors* was republished as a book, and widely reviewed; it's probably the closest he got to a bestseller. *Land of Ophir*, on the other hand, has never before been reprinted since its appearance in the three March 1922 issues of *Adventure*. It's easy to see why it wouldn't have been picked up by a publisher. It's relatively short at 58,000 words, but still manages to get a bit wordy in its later stages when the reader is eager to neutralize the suspense with action. That aside, readers who love Beadle will love *Land of Ophir*, which takes for its final setting the legendary city of gold and wealth that has never been found. The extended setup of the story evokes the romantic globe-trotting of another day, which may mirror the way in which Beadle spent his younger days. The tale has numerous colorful characters—including Billy Langster, who returns from "The City of Baal" (*Adventure*, January 18, 1921)—and plenty of action, mystery, even horror. *Land of Ophir* captures the weirdness and danger of Africa in Beadle's inimitable fashion.

The Land of Ophir

A THREE-PART STORY
PART 1.

by

Charles Beadle

I'VE OFTEN SUPPOSED THAT THE MAN WHO STICKS IN THE HOME TOWN, or mighty close, commutes, rears babies and goes in for uplift or any other kind of dope the newspapers put over on 'em, think right back in their nuts that we who've been bitten by that unclassified microbe which produces that incurable disease the *Wanderlust*, are more or less crazy. Maybe that's so, as old Hiram said, and then ag'in, maybe it ain't.

But sometimes, when I've bumped into a few of the boys and squatted around a camp-fire or maybe in a saloon on the Barbary Coast—in those wicked old days—I've often wondered whether the home crowd weren't right. For surely they sometimes are a mighty queer mob; can't stand for a nice regular life with the pay-envelope coming in every week, but seem bent on sniffing about for trouble like a coyote after hens. And what's queerer, in the true specimen, he doesn't seem to care a cuss for money.

A scientific guy says that only those who are slightly crazy do any good in the world, and after a spell with a mob of fellow sufferers I like to think of that; makes me get my tail up and stand no back talk from the drug-store clerk.

I recollect one fellow who certainly was bug-house—a Scot who had a claymore and said he was King Robert Bruce and wandered around carving up native tribes because he opined it made him feel good; another who foot-padded and sailed around the world because he believed in finding out things for himself and really wanted to know whether the world was round; Barney Topper, who became a Buddhist *bonze* because he allowed he didn't like working for his grub; and then Billy Langster, who dug up a bunch of forgotten Phenicians, tried to start an empire, and nearly got eaten for his pains.

And have you ever noticed how schoolmates change when they grow up?

You bump into them years after; and an embryo pirate has become a pastor, and the clever little guy is running a sailors' joint in Shanghai.

I've always had a hunch that Captain Kidd and Jean Lafitte must have been choir boys when they were kids and—it seems like sacrilege—I've wondered what happened to *Huckleberry Finn* and *Tom Sawyer* when they grew up; often couldn't help staring at some tame old guy in a clothes store and wanting to inquire—

"Say, mister, 're you *Huck* or *Tom*?"

There was a fellow like that—I don't mean a *Tom* or *Huck*—at school, who didn't run true to form. Long, lanky ——— he was, with tow hair and sharp, bird-like eyes. He was a regular New Englander and came from Bawston, which was enough to turn anybody against him.

But it wasn't that so much as his darned cleverness. You know the chap who carries off scholarships and all that, and besides has the nerve to be more'n good at sports. That's where he ran up against me; I'll admit that on the other count I was always an also ran.

Fraser Halde Thorpe ran so hard that the result was a row which ended in an enforced draw. After that I couldn't see my way to take him to my bosom; but that was his fault, for he would try to take it out of me by his tongue until I insisted upon another dose of the same medicine. He was game all right, and it took me ten rounds to put him out—not bad going for youngsters—but then at sixteen I had already well developed the physique of my ancestors, one of whom was an admiral who swept the British from the sea with a broom at his mainmast head.

Somehow nobody liked Thorpe; too darned smart with his tongue—and everybody prophesied that he would end as a bum on the Barbary Coast. We passed out about the same year, he going, as he would, to Harvard. My folks had gone to live in California by then. I guess some old microbe had already bitten me, or the old admiral had broken loose. Dad wanted me to go to Cornell or Princeton if I liked, but I couldn't see it.

I got as far as New York and then—*kismet*, as the Arabs say, shanghaied me on board a windjammer bound for Canton. Those were the old days of bucko mates when they hove the old horse overboard and sang "Whisky Johnny." I left the *Charity Wetfield* there because I couldn't stand for the old man's idea of charity with a belaying-pin.

He was a nephew of the owner, and thought he could do what he liked, and was as wet as the old tub in dirty weather. I shipped out of Canton in a British boat where they weren't such rough-necks, and was six or seven years before the mast, and then I got my ticket.

A year or two after that I met up in Yokohama with a fellow cut in a different shape, one Billy Langster, a crazy guy if ever there was one. He'd just scrambled across in a junk from somewhere in China with a bunch of priests on his heels. He'd been trying to lift the emerald eye of a Buddhist god, so he said. I didn't believe him.

Anyway these thugs surely did try to stick him, and I helped to get him out of an ugly mess in an opium-joint. So I came home at last by way of the Golden Gates. I was out of a berth at the time, but I found one as substitute for the second, who had fallen sick, of the bark *John Lavery*, and took Billy along with me.

Of course the folks wanted me to stop home and be good. I couldn't hope, in a way, for mother to understand, but I did expect dad would. But no, sir. We just looked at each other and sort of seemed as if we'd met for the first time. Queer that. And he'd knocked about a bit as a mining engineer before he married. But I've noticed that dads have a trick of cutting all that stuff out of their memory somehow.

One sister was married and up in Seattle, and the other was just on the point of getting spliced with a solemn guy in San Francisco. An elder brother made it worse for me, as he'd followed the dollar trail as tamely as a burro.

I felt out of it, although I was awful sorry for mother. I was broke, of course. Finally I snaked out of it by promising to go up and see sister, but somehow I lost my way and found myself riding the rods East. I felt rather sore about that; seemed mean. But I couldn't help it; just had to. I managed to get nearly as far as Chi, and then got thrown off. Worked in a packing-house for a bit; drifted to Boston; and shipped again.

Down in the Argentine I got a job to run horses to the Cape. Then I was through with the sea for good. Went with the crowd up to Kimberley, but I was a bit late for the ball; starved and nearly died of thirst, tramping in circles about the Kalahari Desert for three years, and only found one three-carat stone. I've got it still in a stick-pin. After that I quit and went up into Rhodesia.

There I met up with a fellow, an Africander, Ollendorf, whom I'd known down in the Kalahari. He was flush for the moment and grub-staked me for a prospecting-trip. A bit of luck came my way, and I located a likely reef. But that meant expensive machinery, so we sold out to a Bulawayo company and went in together trading. Did mighty well for a bit, and then as there were too many others butting in we decided to trek north, Zambesi way and beyond.

Some months later we pulled into Gwelo and just naturally made for the nearest saloon—the Maxim Hotel, I recollect. As Ollendorf called for swigs of real Montagu *dop* to take the dust of the road out of our mouths I began to stare, for there was something familiar about the lanky figure and tow hair of the barkeep.

As he turned to serve us I caught a certain twist of the head on the neck that started phone bells ringing—Fraser Halde Thorpe!

So vividly did old memories come tingling back that I wanted to laugh.

Thorpe the clever guy, Thorpe the superior person, as a barkeep in a pioneer shanty! Some scholarship! And yet there was something—old times I guess—which brought him round in a different light. I felt tickled to death to see him. At first he didn't seem at all pleased to see me, but he thawed and grinned.

He seemed changed a lot, yet just the same in mannerisms. Of course we had a long *indaba*. Seems he'd smothered himself in glory at Harvard, started in on academic wings as a professor, and then something came over him—he wasn't good at explaining what—and he cut the painter without warning.

"Bully," thought I; "I never thought he was capable of it," and warmed to him, for I understood better than he did himself.

Then he found out that out in the open you couldn't rope a steer with an 'ology, nor did it help any to keep your feet on a gasket at the end of a yard in a southerly gale. He had wandered around really learning things. And here he was, a professor in a bar! And he's not the only one I've met.

Naturally I wanted to do all I could to fix him up. Persuaded him after a lot of trouble to come along with me to Salisbury, where, through relations of my partner, Ollendorf, I got him a job as secretary up at the Kaiser Wilhelm Mine, Urania way.

About a year later we had wandered down after ivory to the northwest of Lake Albert Edward in a district which was—on the map—French territory. At the *kraal* of a chief, with whom we were bartering for porters, occurred another of those little coincidences in life. Another trader—or he said he was—came along and pitched his camp close beside ours. I saw him coming in, and noticed that he had a big number of men in the *safari* carrying nothing; women as well. He came over to look us up, and neither Ollendorf nor I took a fancy to him.

We put him down as a Levantine of some sort—mixture of Greek, Syrian, the Lord knows what, such as Alexandria and the Levant breeds. He had a yellow neck and a curious trick of moving his eyes without moving his head—like a darned lizard. He spoke English fairly well—some of that tribe speak a dozen lingoes "fairly well"—and said his name was Gandy, but he was too slick and cringing for us to have much truck with.

According to his yarn he was bound west looking for ivory, but I had a shrewd suspicion then that the color was black, and anyway he'd come in from that very direction. We gave him a cup of tea and shunted him off.

But about seven that night—almost full moon—there was a —— of a caterwauling from his camp, and a boy came bawling that the "white man" was killing his sister.

"Come on, Olly!" said I. "Get your gun, man, and let's see what this yellow-belly's up to."

Over in his camp, in the light of the fire and moon, among a crowd of jabbering natives, was a woman spread-eagled to a tree and a big black buck laying into her with a *sjambok*. By his side stood little Gandy; evidently conducting operations.

Telling Olly to keep his gun on the Levantine, I covered the big fellow and ordered him to loose the girl. He gave one look and obeyed—*pronto*—amid wild expostulations from Gandy, as he called himself.

"Quit that!" I told him. "Or you'll be mighty sorry. I don't give a —— what the girl's done, but we'll have no rough stuff around while we're here. What's the matter anyway?"

I turned to the girl, who was crouched in a heap with her back in a bloody mess. I asked in Kiswahili—

"Who does she belong to?"

A cowering native in the gloom of a tree answered that they all belonged to the "white man."

Slavery!

That made me madder than ——. I called out, "Keep that little swine covered, Olly;" and added to the natives, "Every man and woman who wants his freedom, let him run for the bush and I will hold this thing which is no 'white man.' "

Gandy broke out into a half a dozen languages, I reckon, in his rage, but the poor devils needed no second bidding. They beat it for all they were worth, and the girl as well.

"You have no right, I tell you!" yelled Gandy. "Thees is my people! We are not in French country! We—"

"I don't care where we are," I retorted "but just get it into your head that no white man will stand for that sort of thing. Get that? Now you'll stop right here for half an hour and then we'll go home, but if you try any tricks you'll start something. Get me?"

But, crazy with rage, he danced right up under my nose shrieking insults until I was compelled to slap his face to bring him to his senses.

And then he did shut up, contenting himself by mumbling curses under Olly's gun, while mine attended to his men. After that we went back to our camp. Although I took the precaution to put out sentries he didn't try any come-back. As a matter of fact the village people knew who he was and would have jumped at a chance, backed up by us, to wipe him out. Next morning he left at sunrise, mighty glad, I think, to get away with a whole skin.

We worked our way slowly, trading and shooting, right up through Tanganyika into Uganda, and did mighty well. Later Ollendorf, who had been badly mauled by a lion and had had several goes of black-water, died of the combination. I was pretty rotten with fever too. I sold out, and then as I could never let well alone I decided to go out by way of the Sudan, after which I would be through with Africa for good. I could afford to be anyway.

But in what is now the Lado Enclave a party of the Mahdi's crowd rushed my camp and wiped out everybody except me, whom they took prisoner—but not before they'd paid mighty dear for the privilege. They kept me around like a bear on a chain for two years and more. In every village or in their own walled towns, they'd stick me in a cage or have me tied while their kids and young men could come and curse, spit on me and make faces like so many monks.

I had some —— of a time, believe me. I can't think about it now without feeling sort of sick in the stomach. Finally I made a break when in the Sudan, and, thanks to my knowledge of their lingoes, got into Kitchener's lines near Khartum. But they surely had mussed me.

When they hoofed me out of hospital after about six months, I went to Italy and made my way slowly back to the Golden State. But I was still such a sick *hombre* that I consented to lay off the trail for good, and that's saying something for the Mahdi bunch!

Guess I might as well admit that a certain little lady with hair like a sunset and blue eyes like the Indian Sea had assisted at the regeneration. You bet the old folk were mighty pleased.

I bought a ranch down in Kings County and started in being good and pretty. And did for some five years—although I'll admit on the square I did get my feet itchy pretty frequently and made a couple of trips down to Mexico.

Then the third inevitable came along, and my partner left me. I put the kids with the old folk and trekked back to Mexico. From there I drifted into a couple of Venezuelan rebellions; got punctured several times, but cleaned up a lump of dough which I didn't particularly need.

Some time later I was in New York City about some business in Tampico. On Broadway I bumped into a fellow I had known slightly down in Mexico—an Englishman, and a good boy in a tough corner but not overstocked with gray matter. Anyway I took him to grub. We found ourselves in the Tenderloin, where we raised a first-class riot. Some smart Alec tried to lift my raw stone for which I'd sweated so mighty hard in the Kalahari Desert for three years. He got what was coming, and then some. Then the gang started the rough stuff.

Hardwicke somehow got separated, and after a lively five minutes I saw that they had him down in a corner. I waded in all spraddled out and got him away, but by the time the argument was over we were both well mussed up.

Anyway next day while we were licking our wounds in a decent feeding-joint he got kind of communicative—sort of out of gratitude I suppose.

Talked a lot of hot air about something he was sworn to secrecy about, but I guess I know how to make a man come through. There were several other *hombres* mixed up in the scheme, which sounded suspiciously like a piratical outfit. It was all connected with a mysterious yacht and Africa.

I reckoned I knew something about yachts and Africa too. It smelled mighty good to me. Next day at any rate he made an awful fuss as to what he had said, but I insisted, and he consented to make me meet the big noise.

That evening Hardwicke took me to a well-known restaurant, where, seated in the shadow of a table lamp, was a well-groomed, fair man, dolled up in evening clothes.

He shook hands with Hardwicke and the latter began—

"I say, I want to introduce you to Mr. Philip—"

But I had caught a glimpse of the hard-cut face and the green, cat eyes and exclaimed—

"Bill, by glory!"

II

"OH," BILLY DRAWLED QUIETLY, "so it's Phil Tromp. Sit down, old-timer, and tell where you came from anyway."

That was just like Billy. But I was rather peeved that his greeting was so cool. On that homeward trip from Yokohama in the *John Lavery* I had rather cottoned to him, although I only half-believed the hints of yarns he'd tell sometimes during a dog watch. He had changed much in the years, and he flattered me, with a twinkle in his eye, that I hadn't; but I knew better, for the Mahdi gang had seen to that.

He ordered cocktails much as if we were just sort of signaling in passing; but I saw by a sharp, interrogative glance at his henchman, Hardwicke, that he was wondering whether I knew anything or not. We talked reminiscences during dinner. When I casually referred to my wanderings in Africa I noticed that he pricked up his ears. I sketched my days since, but he didn't respond in kind.

I began to get impatient, yet I didn't want to give Hardwicke away. Presently, with the coffee and a liqueur, I butted in with an indirect hint.

"Now say, Billy," said I, "what game are you up to now? Haven't any more eyes of a Buddhist god in view, have you?"

Billy lighted a cigar with care, smiled vaguely and replied—

" 'Smatter of fact I have—this time it isn't Chinese."

"Where is it now—Alaska or the Andes?" I inquired blandly, smiling at Hardwicke. "I want something hot, for I've never been able to stand the cold since the Mahdi toasted my toes."

"Say," said he after a long pause, regarding me solemnly, "d'you believe in predestination?"

"Holy glory!" I exclaimed, gulping; for I'm not accustomed to freight words, except in books. "What on earth d'you mean?"

"Nothing. I was just thinking. From what you hinted of your trail since I left you on the Barbary Coast you are the one man I've been praying for."

Hardwicke looked relieved, and I began to feel that I really liked Billy. He looked at his cigar ash meditatively.

"You're a crazy guy, Phil," said he. "That's why I prayed for you. Bit rusty, but I prayed mighty hard, believe me. That, and your African experience. Say—know the patter a bit, huh?"

"You bet. Arabic, Kiswahili, Sintebili, Madingo, Ewe—or I used to; and I guess I could rub 'em up a bit."

"Good. I remember you surprised me by the way you slung the chink talk—almost as well as I did myself in those days. I'm not great, for one thing, on northern lingo, although I can sling it a bit. It's Africa this time."

"Ah," said I loyally, "so maybe I'll call in on some of my old pals."

"Sure, I hope so. It's around that way. Say, let's go to the lounge. I'm not used to hunching up straight like a fakir with an arm up. Smells stuffy and stale to me, all this. I've been in this burg for three weeks too long, and, oh, boy! I'm just that thirsty for a real man's land."

He called for the bill, and we went to Billy's room. When we were comfortably housed with the usual fixtures Billy, sitting on his shoulders sucking a cigar, began.

"After I left you on the Barbary Coast, as broke as you were, I too went off to see my folk and tried to be good. But nothing doing. I drifted up to li'l ole New York one bright day and fell across a dopy guy in an opium-joint down the Bowery, who told me such a crazy yarn that I lied like a greaser and got an uncle to grub-stake me for planting in Ceylon or the Andes—I've forgotten where—but it worked enough dough to carry me off to East Africa.

"There I got in with a bunch of prehistoric guys who had been intimate pals of Adam or nearabouts, running the oldest religion in the world. Snaked my way in, and—by the Lordy!—became pretty nigh chief priest. Got an English fellow in with me, Faxen, a good sport. We both got darned nigh eaten, but in the end cleaned up a tidy boodle in gold vases and shields and other junk.

"After that, Faxy went home. Never seen him since. But after a joy ride round the States I started in to finance a scheme to corner the opium trade in China and dropped every red cent. Never touch China again. No, sir. Don't seem lucky for me somehow. Then I fooled around in Peru. Came darned near having to work for my grub—you know what I mean—would have if I hadn't taken to the road and hiked across into Brazil.

"On the way those darned Indians nigh got my handsome head for a

miniature to sling in their huts. Then I struck some emeralds and went back
to Africa again—up in Morocco—and tried my hand at making sultans.
Might have had the country as a sort of sun-porch, but the European powers
were so mighty prejudiced. Anyhow that's how I hit the trail for this outfit.
Say, did you ever drop across Johnny Starleton at Alkazar?"

I hadn't, yet I felt rather peeved in admitting the fact. I always regret, as
a matter of fact, that I haven't been in every spot on earth; sort of get sore if
I have to admit publicly that I haven't yet been in ——. You know the sort
of feeling.

"But of course you wouldn't," continued Billy, "as he's never been farther
from Morocco than Gib. Think he's a rock scorpion, although his brother,
Freddy, claims to be an American citizen. Anyway Johnny's quite a big noise
around there. He speaks Arabic like a native—better than English—at least I
hope he does! Fat! Looks like an amiable Buddha. In with all the Moors and
has land and does a thriving trade in the protégé game.

"You know, if a Moor is in partnership or in the employ of a Britisher or
Frenchman, he can claim protection and exemption from any little fads the
sultan or local *kaids* think up. Johnny has dozens, and a quarter or more of
each one's property as consideration. Oh, he's some wise guy! I ran into him
on the king-making business. Half came in, but the sly bird knew too much,
I guess.

"Anyway through him I met up with another regular fellow, an Irish lord
without any bucks who'd been trying to wangle some concession down south
from a big chief, Ma-el-Einen. This fellow's a *shareef*—holy man—who
claims descent from Mohammed. There're millions of 'em, but he's a kind
of pope—doesn't even pay tribute to the sultan. 'Smatter of fact, the boot's
on the other leg, for the sultan pays him—to keep quiet down in the Sûs.

"Fieldmorre got the concession, but signed only by deputy—anyway
the whole scheme was mussed by political jealousy—same as me. France,
England and Germany are all sitting round with their tongues lolling out,
with one eye on Morocco and the other on each other.

"He reckoned to break in at Cape Juby away below Agadir on the border
of the reputed Spanish territory. He'd already been down there and done
some trading in a small way, but the great idea was to start a base station
there and another in the interior, and tap the great caravan route from the
Sudan and the Congo, which passes through the country.

"The idea had been begun before, Fieldmorre told me, and showed me
the documents. The whole scheme was started by an old Syrian, whom
Fieldmorre stumbled upon in London, when looking for a teacher of Arabic.
This Sabah as a youth had found the place—how I don't know. Anyway he
did, and came to London with a great yarn of the riches in mica, wool, ivory
and gold.

"A dozen got together and formed a syndicate; dubbed themselves the Gentlemen Adventurers. They bought some old tub and started off. But before they'd got farther than Lisbon, seasickness took the guts out of six of 'em and they quit cold. The other six heroes and the Syrian plunged on recklessly; but when they got to the Cape Verde three more got cold feet and were yelling for their mammies. Some adventurers! Reminded me of the nursery rime about 'Twelve little nigger boys sitting in a row!'

"The remaining three and Sabah the Syrian interpreter and promoter put into Lanzarotte to establish a base, took a deep breath and dived for Juby. It appears that first they got along fine. An Arab chief loved 'em like brothers and was tickled to death at the idea of bringing nice woolly lambs into his district. They signed treaties and The Lord knows what. The chief gave 'em a bit of rock, on which they built a fort-factory, and his protection from desert nomads. They started in to do mighty well, apparently.

"The only he-man of the party seems to have been a Scot with a hard head. As long as he was there things ran like a ferryboat. He saw the possibilities and wanted to go up-country, so he left for home to dig up more capital from the other nine pirates sitting in their clubs in Pall Mall, and left a young stiff in charge named Wilkins with Sabah. 'Smatter of fact Sabah was the whole goods, particularly from the chief's point of view; blood brother and so on; spoke the lingo perfectly.

"But Wilkins, left alone, thinks he's a —— of a noise and insisted on running the show. Before, they had always gone ashore to trade; but now this dry-goods young man got cold feet, wouldn't listen to Sabah, and refused to budge off the rock, which kind of hurt the old man's feelings, I guess.

"After that the natives wouldn't—or seldom would—come near the fort to trade; probably they were sulky. Wilkins wanted to send insulting and threatening messages, but Sabah wouldn't translate 'em. Then one fine day he takes himself by the pants and drags himself ashore, presumably to give the chief a calling down.

"As luck would have it, a party of interior Arabs drifted in on a raid. Wilkins beat it to his rock, saying his prayers, and began firing on every one within sight on the beach. Sabah in disgust wanted to resign, but he couldn't get away, as their lugger was over at Lanzarotte at the time, where the other stiff was in charge of the base, who was also, from all accounts, a prize boob.

"At any rate, after the riot was over, the chief, who seems to have been a mighty good sport, sent to the fort, explaining that the attackers were some of the nomad tribes who had got out of hand, but that nothing serious had been intended. This handsome apology the Wilkins boob, who had shot up some of the sheik's own men, refused to accept, maintaining that it was a plot to trap him ashore and slit his worthless throat.

"From Sabah's account they remained shut up and isolated from the shore, firing wildly at anything that approached in a boat, while Wilkins sent frantic letters when the lugger came, reporting that they were besieged by thousands of wild Arabs or some such nonsense and begging for a British gunboat!

"This cheery news came just at the time that the Scot had persuaded the syndicate to come across with some dough. Just naturally they closed up like a clam, and although history don't relate the fact I shouldn't be surprized if they fortified Pall Mall and assembled the British Navy. What they did do was to work things with their government to terrify the sultan—who had no more power or property there than I have in Kansas City—into buying the store on the rock for a quarter of a million perfectly good bucks with warships and admirals to collect it! Fact! Some put-over, the scuts!"

"But what's happened since?"

"Listen and I'll tell," reproved Billy. "That outfit was somewhere around thirty years ago or so. As I said, Fieldmorre had been down there with an old Syrian Sabah, trading in a small way—he it was who got up-country to Ma-el-Einen and got Fieldmorre's concession, and at the time when I butted in he was figuring on making another run. We chipped in. The fort's still there—or the ruins—mostly inhabited by a son of the old sheik, whose men Wilkins shot up. He wasn't over-pally when we came. Probably, I thought, he recollected stories of his father and wondered whether the fort was fool-proof.

"But the real trouble had been that Fieldmorre had on the last trip fallen foul of his idea on morals. A French crew had been wrecked there, and some of his men who don't seem to love the French, reckoned it was a good opportunity to get even a bit by cutting their throats; lined 'em up on the beach with that amiable intention.

"Fieldmorre just naturally couldn't stand for that. He got the sheik aboard by a ruse, then put a gun to his *jelab* and asked him politely how many houris he reckoned he was going to meet within the next few minutes, or words to that effect.

"The sheik reconstructed his system of ethics, but he had evidently remained sore about the affair on account of his loss of face with his people. Then Fieldmorre figured it would be good to have a change of air for a while. With his Irish sense of humor he had forgotten to mention this small entanglement.

"Anyway, after a lot of powwow, and Sabah's influence, we bought his good-will and did a little trade; filled up the lugger with stuff and made several runs to Lanzarotte. Neither of us had much cash to play around with, so we couldn't do anything big. I decided I'd rather go into the interior than fool around in a small way. Fieldmorre was game. So we sent back the boat to the islands.

"But when we broached the matter to the Sheik Abu Matla he warned us in his long-winded, Oriental way that he would not be responsible to the British or French Government for us—he had a holy terror of warships since a talkee-talkee after the ship-wrecked-sailor outfit—and any non-Mohammedan going into the interior usually ended in one of the various fancy deaths which they're so good at inventing. However, naturally we weren't to be put off and by means of stuff in kind and larger promises Sabah got him to provide us with animals and men to take us as far as the big boss, the Shareef Ma-el-Einen.

"We had several little brushes with nomads, but nothing serious, and found the old gentleman a decent sort of guy. He promised to sign any old thing until we shoved the papers under his nose, and then came such a cross-fire of 'ifs' and 'buts' and 'hows' and 'whys' that there was nothing doing for weeks. In the meantime we kept our eyes skinned, and while Fieldmorre and Sabah did the powpow I sweated up the lingo.

"Pour me out another, Hardwicke, there's a good boy. Talking makes me as dry as that darned desert. Go on, Phil! Huh? Oh, then before we tried to come to terms with the old boy something butted in that kinder painted the horse another color—a small Frenchman named Vèron, who spoke Arabic like a native. He drifted in one day with a caravan from the French Senegal and was making his way to Tlemcen, exploring and mapping, and so into Algeria.

"He was a sporting little guy with a pug nose and a dense red beard and eyebrows, and we were mighty glad to see him there. As we had some canned stuff and he was living Arab he dined with us. Talking afterward with Fieldmorre, who slings French like one of 'em—I can't unfortunately—he kinder loosened up and started relating his adventures.

"But when Fieldmorre told him where we figured to make for he went right up in the air. You know what a —— of a fuss a Frenchie's liable to make. I caught a few of the words. 'Imposseeble!' he kept on crying, and something about suicide. The rest I couldn't get until Fieldmorre interpreted.

"To cut it short, he sang tenor to the Sheik Matla's bass: Sure as death and all that sort of stuff; suicide to attempt the trip without a powerful column. Some mysterious tribe away beyond; every white disappeared; not one but many; several French, a German trader, a Swiss from the Belgian Congo Free State, and an Englishman was the last.

"When we or Fieldmorre politely demurred, Vèron dived beneath his robes—he was in Arab dress of course—and yanked out a dirty parchment-bound book from his *skaarrah*—the kind of leather bag Arabs carry.

" '*V'la! V'la*,' he shouted, and gabbled excitedly.

" 'The captain says,' interpreted Fieldmorre, 'that the last man to disappear was an English explorer; that this book, which is his uncompleted diary, he bought from a coast Fantee who had probably stolen it, thinking that he could get a lot of money for it from a white. The captain wishes us to read it.'

" 'No! No!' exclaimed the Frenchman, staring at me. 'You—must—no. No—good. Keel.' And launched into a voluble explanation.

"Anyway there in the small tent over a hurricane lamp Fieldmorre and I read something which changed our ideas quite a bit."

Billy got up quietly, and, opening a dispatch-box, took out a small book, the binding of which was covered in grubby canvas.

"Read it," said he, "while I get a rest. Guess I'm not used to all this lip-work. Start right there," he added, finding a page three-quarters of the way through. "The other's just ordinary exploration notes from the beginning of the trip."

III

THE CANVAS COVER OF THE SMALL BOOK WAS BATTERED, and looked as if it had been twenty times across Africa. The writing, on lined paper with a margin, was small and crabbed, sometimes in ink and sometimes in pencil, mighty hard to read. The page Billy had indicated opened with this entry:

Oct. 26—Arrived village of Nsonnafo. Tribe: Sunfaso. About thousand inhabitants. Pastoral people; plenty of milk, eggs, etc. Glad to be out of tropical forest country and the humid heat. The chief, from tribal marks, is Mambaziwa, as most of the ruling class seem to be in this country. Very hospitable. Treated me well and afterward seemed very friendly, replying to my inquiries quite freely. Mohammedan, and so are his people; but seem, like so many religions, not to have cast out old tribal superstitions.

Noticed a mark which I think is the symbol of a subphraty of the Snake Society. From what he didn't say I rather surmise that they still practise the pagan rites as freely as ever. Later persuaded him to relate some of the current legends (see Note 257). More curious than usual, and bear every evidence of the totem system corroborated by him. His totem is Sonyaza (*Felis Dawei*) and is therefore forbidden to kill or touch them. Most intelligent. Shall accept his invitation to stay a few days.

Nov. 1—Still at Nsonnafo's. Quite like him. Gave me a shoot; put up bearers and everything splendidly. Brought up a young wife suffering from a tumor; looked suspiciously like a cancerous growth. Wish I knew a little more surgery. Would have loved to operate. Lanced and dressed it, which seemed to give her much relief. Old man very grateful; wanted me to accept a whole tusk, but I can't spare porters.

Next day he became more communicative and has opened up considerably;

talked a lot about the country and boasted about himself. Says that he is a descendant as far as I can make out of the Ethiopians (which quite possibly may be true as there always has been a great influx from the East all over the Sudan—this is, strictly speaking, the Sudan) and talks about a great empire bigger than the white man's which was called in the time of his great ancestors O-feer (sounds like Ophir; but this is ridiculous, as the land of Ophir from which Solomon got his gold was thought to be in Arabia but has recently been proved to be Zimbabwe in southern Mashonaland, the Phenician ruins. May be a reference to the empire of Melle, which in the 17th century was of vast extent from the Nile to the Gold Coast. Must try to find origin of this name O-feer. Curious!) I asked him where the empire was now, but he said abruptly that he didn't know.

Seems to grasp reason for my questions. Had long conversation. Astonishing hold of what one almost may call philosophy; propounded curious scheme based (I think. Look up details) on Berber cosmogony. Gave me a whole heap of native folk lore (see Note 261). Very valuable, as I hadn't come across any similar record.

Nov. 8—Nsonnafo, begging me to stay for indefinite period, wants me to become blood brother, thanks to the lucky chance of my surgical attempt; wife doing splendidly. When talking about supplies, which he wishes me to accept without payment, I asked what sort of country was to the northeast. He said, "Bad." I inquired if any whites had been up there. He said distinctly that several had gone there.

When I asked whether they had come back this way, the manner in which he replied that they had not—"none at all"—awoke my suspicions that he was keeping back something—that, and the insistent invitation to stay or return to the coast. Rather wish I could afford the time, particularly as he's such a good sort, but mainly because of my suspicions. Smacks of something to do with tabu.

Nov. 10—Made two days' good march. Country fairly good going, rolling uplands, grass and bush; plenty of game; many small villages belonging to Nsonnafo; nights quite pleasantly cool immediately after sunset.

My suspicion was correct. Before leaving, Nsonnafo, after much beating about the bush, advised me not to continue as the country was dangerous; under pressure said that two whites had gone up there—a German and a Frenchman as far as I could make out—but had died there; how, I could not get a hint from him. I told him that we whites were not in the habit of turning back because of danger—seemed rotten thing to say, but one has to remember prestige and the native mind.

He closed up after that until I was bidding him good-by. Then without direct reference to the previous warning he presented me with a charm hung on a native-worked gold chain, which he mentioned casually would preserve me from the evil spirits on the road. As I thanked him he added that he wished me to leave a piece of nail or some of my hair with him. I replied solemnly that I should be delighted to please him and asked why he wanted it.

"So that my doctor may enchant it and that your soul (of the head) will come to dwell in my country," he replied.

This from a professed Mohammedan! Mohammed would have had a fit, but it corroborates my idea that they retain all the old pagan practises and beliefs. But, good Lord, if one were to be put off by every African superstition one wouldn't get farther than Accra! Ridiculous, but very interesting, bless the old boy!

After that, for several pages came ordinary entries about the country and the villages he was passing through. Then this:

Nov. 21—Came down six hundred and ninety feet in the last five days. Country becoming more tropical and temperature mounting in ratio. Uninhabited. Last village learned no natives for ten days and that they were "bad." Probably means vigorous, warlike tribe who raid them; pastoral and agricultural tribes always say that—and with cause—about the others.

Nov. 26—Came most unexpectedly upon arid scrub. Fortunately thought it looked ugly, and so stocked up with water. No more native paths. Steering by compass due northeast.

Nov. 30—Country same, except for fortunate *donga*, where by digging we refilled water-skins. Can see ahead blue of low hills.

Dec. 2—Nsonnafo was surely right. Country bad—looks worse ahead; hills bare gneissic granite; no sign of vegetation nor water last day; sand; not even Cactaceæ or Palmaceæ; no means of estimating how far hills extend. Porters say two days, three days, ten days, one moon; usual reactions to suggestion and fear of white; very uneasy and discontented; going is very hard for them; can't make speed in this infernal sand.

Dec. 5—Seven porters deserted—had to hold remainder with revolver night and day; no sleep for two nights. Today have tied them together. Had to abandon five loads and split up others. In midst of hills, low conical shaped; full of boulders. Fortunately foresaw lack of water and put camp on half-ration at last water, but only enough for two or three days. Hills look interminable. Country looks like what *Macbeth's* blasted heath ought to have looked like.

Dec. 8—Three porters collapsed; had to leave them; water nearly exhausted; one spoonful each for the day. Feel groggy myself; blazing heat of refraction and touch of malaria (temp. 101). Suppose was a bit light-headed;

cursed because I couldn't shoot those poor souls and put them out of their misery; others staggering; want to lie down and die; feel like a slave-driver.

Desert of sand, limestone, shale, Paleozoic. No sign of break in infernal country. Forced abandon all loads except instruments, guns, ammunition, canvas boat, some food and medicine; divided loads into quarters for each man. Heat awful—119 degrees shade—no shelter.

Dec. 11—Four more porters caved in; had force on others by threatening to shoot (queer reaction—desire to die yet frightened of gun) water finished; no break . . . groggy . . . seem walking in circles.

Dec. 12—Serious. Abandoned instruments, everything except little food and trade goods and medicine; another two dropped; one went mad; saw him running up a hill; tried to shoot; poor devil.

Dec. 13—Escarpment; forest below; porters bucked up, struggling gamely.

Dec. 16—Descended some hundreds of feet, but can not record as have no instruments. —— nuisance. . . . Forest dense. . . . Am resting beside small river; no sign of inhabitants. One porter died last night of exhaustion apparently; probably drank too much water. Signs of plenty game about, but too done up to go out yet. Still have slight fever. Intend stay another two days, get men fit. Bit depressed; think really because instruments all gone. If have any luck by meeting friendly people, will try persuade them to go back and pick up goods and recover instruments.

Dec. 17—Camp rushed dawn; sentry either asleep or surprised; every one massacred except myself for some reason. Natives mixed; some negroes, others Fulani type and all robed Arab fashion, armed mostly long-bladed spears, swords and good many guns—Belgian Sniders. Promptly looted all gear left; saved this diary as it happened to be in my *skarrah*; that, revolver, knife, pocket compass, sketching-pad, pencils and empty pen is all I have.

Leader dressed better than others. Fulani type but speaks Arabic well; can understand dialect; related to Mandingo.

Leader refused answer questions save that I am to be taken before local chief in whose village I am now. Houses mud and wattle after Arab fashion but better constructed than any seen south. This house of chief, of stone and mud; furnished grass mats; carved stools; and much woven and dyed cloths.

Haven't succeeded in extracting any information of what they intend to do with me. Call themselves Mazatlanzi. Evidently only lower classes negroid wear any tribal cicatrices; probably slaves raided from south; noticed on lintel of this house sign of Snake Society. Inference probably Nsonnafo belongs subphraty and dared not reveal what he knew; hence his well-meaning hints. . . . Fortunately feel normal again.

Dec. 19—Haven't had an opportunity to make entry as have been on *safari* and dare not openly write for fear they may force me to give up book, thinking, native fashion, that I am making magic. Saw chief next day. Fair and red-haired. Certainly Berber origin. Very courteous. Asked innumerable questions, to some of which I replied; others I refused.

Curious beast. Reminded me of some one, but I can't think who. Noticed that before, by the way; natives frequently remind one in some curious way of Europeans one knows or has met.

Well dressed in Arab fashion; jeweled dagger sticking ostentatiously out of his *jelab*; embroidered shoes—not on him, of course, but outside the door—worked after the Moroccan pattern. Lives well too.

Offered kind of Oriental sweets and splendid coffee. When I protested against the massacre of my men and asked what the —— they meant by making me a prisoner, he reacted in the Oriental way by ignoring my questions, and when I pointed out the danger of being impolite to a white man he smiled slightly—the beast! But I couldn't get one single bit of information save that I was to be taken to the city of the sultan . . . —— irritating; but in playing this game with Orientals one has to have the patience of Sisyphus.

Dec. 24—Mambakzino. Am arrived at the capital, and the residence of the sultan. Certainly was astonished, and have been ever since leaving the first village. From there runs a broad, made road (no record of this in Africa before European influence save Uganda—true, there is evidently extensive Arabian influence). Each village passed—and some were almost towns relatively—were walled and quartered after the true Arabian fashion. Noted many fair; some red-haired; Berber origin, as the first chief was; evidently the aristocracy.

Left dense forest first day; rolling, park-like country; probably about five thousand feet, judging roughly since I lost altimeter; evidently rich soil and looks auriferous, although I had no opportunity to examine; seemingly corroborated by the quantity of gold bangles worn by the nobility (another point; as with Nsonnafo's people they are Mohammedans; but don't observe strictly). Palm-wine is also drunk, I remarked. Much cultivation; observed cotton, coffee, indigo, maize, rice, plantains, bananas, cassava, millet.

Certainly was astonished by the size of the capital; estimate must contain somewhere about seventy or eighty thousand inhabitants—if not more. Remarked that here houses nearly all built of stone and mud, with large courtyards and gardens. Find this remarkable so far south. Noticed, too, passing through the streets, few modern rifles: Lee Enfields, Mannlichers, Winchesters, as well as many Martini Sniders.

Didn't have an opportunity to see much of the town as they brought me straight here—in a hammock, for which I was very grateful, for I've got a temperature again. Don't know what, as these swine have stolen my medicine-chest.

Noted several mosques. City sprawls rather pleasantly over several small low hills. . . . Saw in garden the largest monitor lizards I've ever seen, some quite six feet or more long.

Am lodged, I believe—for I can't make any of them talk and have nothing to bribe them with—in the sultan's palace, for I entered through very thick walls—didn't look very old, which I thought was odd—into a house which appeared to be in the center of large gardens, with terraces, as far as I could make out, somewhere beyond. . . .

There's a bright moon tonight, and through the large window, barred, the gardens look very beautiful, filled with a warm, spicy odor. I'm to see the sultan tomorrow. . . .

I meant to write more tonight, the first chance to be alone for some few days, but I feel fed up and irritated, and my head's like a —— balloon with malaria.

Dec. 25—Am scribbling this in antechamber of sultan. Dragged me out at sunrise; appeared to be in some sort of hurry. Wonderful gardens; never saw anything like them. Window overlooks. Everybody here seems to be Berber origin, nobles I presume. Dressed magnificently; jewels in their turbans and swords. Guards gigantic negroes—probably slaves from West Coast.

Palace certainly is Oriental; most luxurious. This room not very big but lofty; walls, doors, ceiling, floor, made of planks like a parquet, of ivory, with gold setting between, cemented as it were; two low divans in watered silk—looks to me like a product of the House of Liberty—on one of which I'm sitting. Nothing else.

Curious; this white or rather old-ivory-and-gold room exercises a weird effect. Suddenly recalled Nsonnafo's yarn about his ancestors and the empire of O-feer, and surely the profusion of gold and ivory suggest Ophir. Certainly would be a great joke to prove the pundits wrong about the Zimbabwe. . . .

Later. Just heard bits of curious conversation outside my window—spoken in good Arabic. Something about:

"Sidna is very pleased, for Allah hath surely blessed his ways.

"Great is Allah! For he hath sent a sweetly morsel for our lord O-Seeah-do.

"Who knoweth the will of Allah? Who knoweth whether he be destined for the lords of the forest or the arena?

"Who knoweth the will of Allah!"

Curious. Evidently refers to some pagan practise which, as I've observed in my notes, clings to these Moham . . .

The last sentence was scarcely decipherable; ended in a scratch.

I looked up at Billy and Hardwicke, smoking cigars. Billy regarded me meditatively as if trying to figure out how I was taking it. Then he said with a slightly satirical smile—

"Reckon its genuine?"

"I do, sure."

I stared at the worn little book and reread mechanically the last few words.

"For the love of Mike—have you read this, Hardwicke?" I asked.

"I have, and I'm with Langster until —— freezes."

"Me too," said I, "but—but what happened after—"

"That's what we're going to find out—that and several other things."

"But—who was this guy anyway?"

"Inside the cover," directed Billy.

I pulled back the canvas envelope.

"W-w-w-w-what!" I gasped.

On the parchment cover was printed in copperplate:

FRASER HALDE THORPE

"Frazzy Thorpe! Glory! Of all the—"

IV

"WHY—DID YOU KNOW HIM?" INQUIRED BILLY.

"I was at the same school with him. By glory, sure I know him, and I'll bet he hasn't forgotten me!"

I sat looking at the grubby little book and thought of those friendly scraps with Thorpe. Had Africa got him? If so, here was myself evidently about to ask for the same medicine. Mighty queer!

After all, was it? Stranger coincidences than that in life. Yet I couldn't get rid for some time of a sense of something uncanny—sort of shivery feeling about the spine, as if you were just getting a message from gran'ma on the planchette, telling you to be sure to keep on your flannel underwear, only making you feel funny all the same.

"The little Frenchman had a heap more to say," continued Billy, setting a glass on the table. "He went on jabbering to Fieldmorre, and I had to sit and cuss. After reading that diary he just naturally wanted to find out what there was to it. He was a sporting little guy—that's why he let us have the diary—and wanted to go and look himself. But he was on duty, and, as he insisted, he knew too much about the country to try out fool tricks on his own. 'Smatter of fact, his attitude convinced us, and that's why we abandoned the trip right there and came back to hunt up the sinews of bloody war, as they say, if that bunch up there really want it."

"But didn't he try to get a line on how the Fantee got hold of this diary?" I inquired.

"Sure he tried. What he didn't know about natives wasn't worth knowing, but all the same he didn't get much. The man said he'd gotten it way up among the Mandingo; insisted that he had bought it from a Hausa. Probably he had stolen it, as I suggested before; yet from what the diary says that might have been possible. One of the negro guards he talks about might have stolen it and deserted.

"However, later he did get some more information—not about your friend or the diary, but about this mysterious tribe. He palled up with an Arab, who thought he was a genuine Mohammedan too—I told you he talks the lingo like a native; that's his job anyway—and from him got a long-winded story.

"The tribe, so the man said, are an offshoot of the Mandingo, but were conquered a long while ago by a mysterious band of Berber nomads, which, according to Vèron, sounds weak, as they are not in the habit of giving up nomading, as it were."

" 'Even as you and I,' " I quoted, and added, "Once a nomad always a nomad!"

"That's right. However, until about five or six years ago they weren't particularly powerful or organized, until the coming of a kind of Messiah, according to this Arab—one who was prophesied, one of whom O-Seeah-do had said, '*Na me yo ko!*' "

" 'He is a son of my flesh,' " I translated. "I'm not so rusty as I thought I was. Ewe lingo I guess. But what's the O-Seeah something? That gets me."

"The Lord of the Snakes."

"That's the same phrase Thorpe mentioned," chipped in Hardwicke, "in that last conversation."

"That's true," I assented.

"To continue," went on Billy after relighting his cigar, "the fellow reported that throughout this country all species of snakes and lizards were sacred; that it was death penalty to kill or touch one."

"Glory!" said I. "I'll cut out alcohol before I get there!"

"Me, too," said Hardwicke, grinning.

"Can it!" snapped Billy. "We wore that joke to rags before we got back to Juby. Anyway the Arab assured the French captain that the Messiah guy had been turned from a snake into a man somewhere in a swamp down south in order to save the country—the usual salvation theory of all races.

"Anyway since his arrival nobody save a Mohammedan or a member of the snake cult had ever returned from the country. What happened to them Vèron couldn't find out, as he wasn't a snakeite an' couldn't give the proper dope. He also—the Arab, I mean—spoke of the extraordinary riches of the country, which corroborated your pal's diary."

"Oh," said I, "probably he's some wise guy who has heard what usually happens when civilization walks in and wants to keep the goods for the people, meaning himself—and I don't know that I blame him."

"Still it seems a pity, with such a lot of deserving people about," commented Hardwicke slyly.

"I guess I'm with you," agreed Billy, smiling. "But to go on. This is about all he could get out of that Arab, but as he came farther north he got hints here and there—evidently as Thorpe did from that chief he was so fond of. Perhaps the Frenchman passed through the same village. Most of the yarns were legendary, but probably based on some sort of fact—a sort of balled-up Mohammedan theology and native folk lore.

"One, which he told us, was that a long time ago—once-upon-a-time business—a son of Mohammed was sent by Mohammed to convert all the tribes of Africa. He traveled through the North successfully proselytizing, where he took for his second and favorite wife—apparently the first lady had stopped home—a daughter of the Berbers, who had a son by him. They came on south, and as they were passing through a dense forest they were set upon by demons.

"When the fight was desperate and the demons had captured the girl and the kid, and were about to kill the old man, an enormous serpent appeared and called out to know what was the trouble. Might have seemed an unnecessary question, but I guess the old man was too busy to notice that.

"Anyway when the great snake had gotten it into his head he offered to rescue the wife and child on condition that he permit him to swallow him. The Shareef O-Seeah-do accepted the terms and was duly swallowed. Mighty queer how all these legends resemble each other; get the same ideas like the flood and Adam and Eve balled up. Ever noticed it?

"The old guy was swallowed and the lady and the boy went on happily ever after, and he or she—these legends are never very clear on matrimonial matters—became the founder of the Mazatlanzi race—that is why to kill or even touch the snakes is tabu, for clearly their ancestor, O-Seeah-do, was inside him or them; that is why, Vèron found out, they call the lord of snakes after him.

"However, some time after, some sort of a local Billy Sunday made a prophecy that O-Seeah-do would come back again in the form of a man, to regenerate the race, in which apparently the pastor guy had the luck, for sure enough shortly afterward appeared the present sultan—á la Jonah—from the belly of a snake."

"Interesting," said I, "like those Mahdi yarns. But what about the Ophir stunt? Did he get any line on that?"

"No," said Billy with a grin, "and we didn't want him to either. He's white all right, but he might talk when he's full of wine back in Paris. Fieldmorre's a hog on ancient lore—Royal Geographical and all that—and I know a little myself. Your friend Thorpe, in spite of his professorship, is off the trail—I mean as far as Zimbabwe goes.

"Lately it's been pretty conclusively proved by Randall MacIver that Zimbabwe is quite a sucking infant—merely three or four hundred years old—in comparison to what she'd have to be to run for these honors, and also that there isn't, and never was, enough gold to have fitted up old Solomon and Company's wholesale orders. The Arabian theory was busted long ago.

"Now, where's my thimble and the pea? Guess where it is. Look at the situation of our empire. 'Scuse me, gentlemen, if I'm a bit previous! In the Sudan and right at the back door of Egypt; probably the land of Punt, of which their records talk a lot of gold and ivory, ostrich-feathers and slaves. That's good enough for me to take a chance on anyway."

"Glory!" said I. "The way you talk you'd convince a man from Missouri! But I'm with you. Any old way we've got to dig Thorpe out. But who's the president of the outfit now? We don't seem to get any farther as to discovering who the fellow is?"

"That's true, but it doesn't seem to matter much who he is," returned Billy. "Our sole concern was how we could get in."

"Wonder your captain didn't have a shy as he could sling the lingo like a native."

"I told you," snapped Billy, as if I were impugning the courage of his friend, "that he wanted to; but besides being on duty he wasn't plumb dippy, and neither were we. You've had enough African and other experience, Phil, to know the difference between a fool stunt and taking a chance. He was no tenderfoot, Vèron.

"I got a hunch that he was right, and so did Fieldmorre. Sabah wanted to go on, and as a Syrian and a genuine Mohammedan—although he'd quit practising—he might have got away with it; but we decided that he was too valuable to risk at that stage. He's scouting around the Ma-el-Einen country now, and he's due at Juby in September."

"All right, don't get sore, Billy," I returned. "It's no use butting into an outfit like this without getting things straight. What about Vèron?"

"Vèron didn't succeed in getting any further information that was of any practical use except by way of the persistent corroboration of all the scraps of yarns he picked up, fairly showing that there's something to it. We decided to quit, and made suitable excuses to old man Ma-el-Einen with a view to keeping in with him; promised him a whole bunch of guns and junk from England, as he'll be very valuable unless he gets fresh at the sight of our little outfit. He might do that through sheer scare, thinking we were trying to put something over on him. We've foreseen that and intend to provide for misunderstandings."

"Would be darned awkward," I commented; "for if he did, our lines of communication with Juby would be closed, wouldn't they?"

"More or less, but we'll have to chance that. We could get out, or perhaps establish a base farther south, between Juby and Porto El Oro, if necessary. Fieldmorre told me there's lots of convenient lagoons around there, although it wouldn't be as convenient as Juby."

"But what about Thorpe? You don't know for sure that he's gone under?"

"Don't for sure. But it looks mighty like it. Vèron was dead positive. None of the others ever came out. Look at the date when the last entry in the diary was written. Two years and more."

"Darn it!" I objected. "I disappeared for thundering nigh three years along with my Mahdi friends."

"Maybe. Perhaps this school pal of yours is doing similar stunts."

"Hope not," said I feelingly. "Rather know he's dead, poor ——. Anyway if he is, I reckon we ought to have a shy at pulling him out of the muss."

"And the others," chipped in Hardwicke.

"You bet! But—say, who's in this outfit beside you two?"

"Fieldmorre, Vèron and Sabah. Fieldmorre's hunting dough and a boat on the other side."

"How much do you reckon you want?"

"About fifty thousand dollars. But we haven't got it all yet. Mighty difficult to get folk to cough up yellow-backs without seeing something tangible—figures, samples, diamonds or something."

"Sure, I know lots come from Missouri. How much are you shy?"

"About twenty thousand."

"I can throw that in. Now, what's the plan?"

"Dig up some good boys—about a dozen whites, I reckon; and recruit a bunch of Hausa—about a couple of hundred. Good scrappers and well disciplined. Have to be done quietly, else we'll get consuls and other inquisitive folk shoving their noses in. Guns—machine and rifles—Fieldmorre's practically fixed on the other side. Load 'agricultural machinery and pianos' for the West Coast.

"He's got an option on a fore-and-aft schooner, thousand gross tonnage, which will suit us fine. Load in England, pick up the crowd at Funchal and Las Palmas—and then better perhaps run down first and hunt Hausa here and there. Daren't try for the whole bunch in one port."

"But," I objected, "how in thunder d'you think you're going to clear the ship from an English port—"

Billy grinned.

"Leave that to me, old dear. She'll sail under the house flag of a regular company, registered and everything, trading between Liverpool and the West Coast of Africa. The Ophir Empire Exploitation, Exploring, Trading and Mining Company. Articles of association drawn up. Wonderful word that, 'exploitation'—covers every mortal thing you can think of from hawking boot-laces to pinching empires. That's to cover all contingencies, and the other two to put 'em off the trail. Offices, 145 Water Street, Liverpool. Got board table, chairs, a typewriter and an office girl. Directors: The Right Honorable Viscount Fieldmorre, F.R.S., F.R.G.S., R.N.R."

"Glory!" I exclaimed. "Sounds like a broadside from a British dreadnought!"

"Good as. We'd have had it American 'cept for that darned Monroe doctrine. Might give somebody a chance to pull Uncle Sam's own stuff on him. Then there's plain me, Hardwicke here, you and Sabah—Vèron, I had to let him in, naturally. He's going to get twelve months' vacation and join us. Useful man anyway—but for professional reasons he can't appear in the directorate. With your whack of dough we'll control the board; and you'll control us, I guess. Tomorrow I'll send a cable to Fieldmorre, and in twenty-four hours the good ship *Penguin* will be in commission."

"Why don't you charter a boat?"

"Thought of that. Too dangerous. Have to have complete control. 'Sides, we'll have to be a registered company for political protection. Doped all that out from what I fell into over the Temple of Baal and the Moroccan concession. If you don't, then Britain or France will just swallow you whole."

"That's true, I guess. But what about your skipper? You'll have to find some one who won't blab."

"Fieldmorre's skipper as well as president. Has an extra-master's ticket, and moreover he's lieutenant in the R.N.R."

Billy grinned.

"Some royal lieutenant, believe me!" he added.

"Say, guess I've a mate's."

"So has Hardwicke here. But yours will be American and no good under the British flag. But we can shove in a dummy and you'll do the work, huh?"

"But what's the idea in going through Juby?"

"As near a route to our country as anywhere else; and it's mighty lonely. Daren't attempt it where gunboats and other craft are monkeying around."

"That's right sure," I admitted. "But what're you going to do, with the old tub while we're busy up-country? Who's going to look after her?"

"Send her home with a scratch crew from the islands and charter her for short voyages. That's what the Liverpool office is for. Six months later, or whenever we wish—we'll have a small lugger at Lanzarotte for mails—she'll be chartered for say Walfisch Bay, report islands, and then hang off Juby for orders."

"Seems you've worked it out some," said I.

"You bet we have," agreed Billy, grinning. "Come fill those glasses, and bottoms up! To the Ophir Empire Exploitation, Exploring, Trading and Mining Company!"

V

AND THE OPHIR EMPIRE EXPLOITATION, EXPLORING, Trading and Mining Company came true all right, as they say in the story books. We spent a fortnight in New York, mostly in Billy's rooms, waiting for telegrams from various boys whom we knew to have more or less the same streak of insanity as we had, coupled, when possible, with some tropical experience, preferably African.

No easy job; for our breed aren't given to correspondence to any extent, not so's you notice, nor to indulging in permanent addresses—and on such an outfit the man may be as rough-neck as he chooses, but he's got to be white all through—no crazy guys who are liable to develop bug-house symptoms in the middle of the desert need apply. Moreover, some fell by the wayside, as it were, and pleaded, as the guests in the Good Book did, that they were going, or mostly had gone, to a wedding feast.

However, we managed, between the three of us, to locate five, in addition to the three whom Billy and Hardwicke had collected before I had butted in. We picked up a couple, but we couldn't afford to waste time by waiting for the others who had to come from Canada and Alaska, so, cabling them the sinews of bloody war and simple instructions to foregather at certain hotels in Funchal and Las Palmas—always wise to keep 'em from talking too much together—we caught the first boat for Liverpool.

Fieldmorre turned out to be a white man, as I might have known he would be if Billy had had anything to do with him. Half-bald, husky fellow, with an Irish nose and eyes, he looked like a Bowery tough with no collar and a cap; some aristocrat. No slouch either. He'd been busy, too.

He'd debated whether to get papers as a private yacht cruising between Great Britain and the southern Atlantic. Heap of advantages in that, and easily fixed for a millionaire or a viscount even when he ain't got money of his own; but "frightfully difficult," as he put it, "to account for unreasonable quantities of pianos, plows and things. One plows the sea and poets talk about the—er—music of the ocean, but— Well, I decided we'd better go in for trade. What do you fellows think?"

'Smatter of fact, as Billy would say, he'd fixed things through the biggest shipping firm running south. Why didn't the Lord give me a title? With a handle to fool the fools and democratic ideas to fool the wise, I'd be emperor of— Oh, ——, I guess I might have had a hop dream around that time.

The *Penguin* was already in commission. We went down to see her. Old, but a darned good sea boat from her lines. I felt an ancient guy as I padded around her, smelling this and that, sea memories coming as thick as the tang from the river. Fieldmorre's eyes twinkled as he saw me watching the large cases being slung aboard right in the middle of Liverpool.

"We hope to develop a large trade in agricultural implements," he remarked dryly.

"Sure," I agreed, "and I guess the west Africans are some music lovers!" eying another great crate swinging on a crane.

I own I got jumpy when the actual time came for clearing-papers; but, as I had hinted, Fieldmorre had fixed that. Titles are useful sometimes in the western hemisphere as well as elsewhere, I've noticed.

Just before feeling the heave beneath my feet—the first for many a long day, for a steam kettle is never the same as a real ship—Billy got a line from Vèron in Paris saying that he was leaving for Mogador, utilizing governmental privileges, and would join us either at Funchal or Las Palmas, or possibly travel overland for the aforesaid reasons—and meet us at Juby.

Yet, honest to goodness, I felt like a kid with a shirt full of apples sneaking out of an orchard until the tug cast off and the halyards began to sing. It was mighty fine, that run out, yarning and trying to work out the future—like a witch-doctor over the guts of a chicken, as Fieldmorre put it—in the cuddy, or pacing the poop. For those who know the breed—I don't give a —— whether he's Eskimo or Fuzzzy Wuzzzy—a man is or he ain't.

The first days on such a venture are as heavy as a pack at the end of a trail; the reaching out, sizing-up of your mates, if you get what I mean. "He travels the farthest who travels alone," I think Kipling said. Yet I guess there was something he didn't know; for of all the fine things right on this little whirling ball we call the earth, the best is a good white pal. Maybe he was right; but I don't know it, and if so it must be mighty like being good—awful lonesome.

Funchal was our first port of call, where we picked up four of the crowd collected in the States; nice boys too; two Irish-Americans, Casey and O'Donnell, a French-Canadian, Poiteau, and a Poliszkwi, a three-generation man.

At Las Palmas, waiting for us on the mole, bless 'em, stiff with boredom, were the other couple, Barnard and Hibbert, two Anglo-Saxons—one man ex-captain and the other a sergeant—suffering from their racial weakness. The six, with the bunch we brought with us—Sarkard and Peters, who'd both sweated and cussed in the Zone and most parts of the tropics; and the four recruited in England, Seeger, a medico, late of the Sudan Service, Broughton and Famitty, who'd seen military service in Nigeria and South Africa, and Pexton, who was a kind of lost soul, a mixture between a naturalist, a botanist and a painter, a small, wiry, swarthy fellow, Welsh I think—made up the dozen.

Hardwicke and Broughton left us for Juby, charged to buy up eighteen riding dromedaries for the white party and Sabah the Syrian, and pack-animals.

As is usual in such cases, a hitch occurred. As we were going to make a run for Accra, where the water is notoriously bad, we decided to fill up our tanks, which held us over for a couple of days.

The first night the officers—that's us—went ashore and trailed up in the tram to the town in search of a dinner—Billy's fault. We had the dinner, but the toasts—considerably later—were interrupted. Do you know Las Palmas? Well—we found the men—they'd had leave; the last, believe me!—in the middle of "the most gorgeous row," as Fieldmorre put it, "as ever happened on the Barbary Coast."

As we entered, the racket was—reminiscent, I guess. I got a vision of the scene.

Our darlings—again Fieldmorre's words—heavily armed with wine-bottles, table legs and chairs, were in joyous mixup with many small people sporting gold lace, knives and a few pistols. Under the kerosene lamp hung from the middle of the dive was our little Welsh painter, botanist etcetera, beating up a stout person entirely surrounded with gold lace and medals.

A little to the right was a hatchet-faced guy sitting on a table like a conductor conducting an orchestra, and on his lap—I blinked; the Spanish wine is mighty strong—was a small kind of dog, looking like a cross between a dachshund and a French poodle.

"Splendid fellows," murmured Fieldmorre admiringly. "This man here," indicating our botanist-painter, "seems quite a useful fellow."

"Maybe you're right, Fieldy," snapped Billy, "but I reckon we'd best close 'em down, just for our own good."

"Me too," said I, "speaking *ex officio*."

How these darn Britishers ruin your speech!

"*Ex officio*," agreed Fieldmorre politely. "I agree with you. You look after our taffy, William, and we'll manage the crew."

Billy—*alias* William—sailed in and caught the naturalist by the shoulders, and, whirling him away from his specimen, jerked the feet from under the incensed *capitano* and deposited him ignominiously upon the floor. This I glimpsed as with Fieldmorre we butted through the jabbering throng toward our own men, swearing good and hard.

As soon as discipline—meaning unreasonable force for the police and reasonable force for our own fold—had restored order, the small guy on the table hugging the small dog butted in.

"Gentlemen," he called out, "I congratulate the British Empire!"

Somehow or other nobody seemed to have noticed him—probably too busy—but the words, strident in the comparative calm, got home.

"Say, mister," yelled a voice, obvious in origin, "is that meaning me?"

Avoiding the authoritative arm of the skipper, out stepped carroty-headed, thickset Casey, and beside him leaped another man as like as his twin.

"Hold yer gob!" shouted O'Donnell. " 'Tis me the lousy ——'s after calling names!"

"That'll do, men," commanded the old man, standing in front of them. "Tromp, old man, just talk to this chap. William, d'you mind bolting that door? Come on you blighters; shut up, and don't be silly! There's plenty of trouble ahead if you want it."

The two Irish glared, rebellion in their eyes. Billy, starting on the way to bolt the door, turned:

"You darned sons o' Saint Patrick an' all his holy angels, don't you know the old man's more Irish than you are? Get out, you scuts!"

For a moment the two stared at Fieldmorre. He smiled while his blue eyes hardened.

"You're drunk, bhoys," he said quietly, "and sure I love ye for it. Will ye be quiet now!"

Then, turning his back on them, he asked me calmly—

"Well, who is this—er—gentleman here?"

As a matter of fact I hadn't taken any notice of the—er—gentleman here. I had been interested solely in a fear that had sprung up of the warring elements among the whites of the expedition, as I had had already experience of such. However, I was now well satisfied that Fieldmorre could play the skipper, and as Casey and O'Donnell grinned and, muttering, stepped back, I knew that all was right; and, turning from our bunch, rediscovered the man with the little dog and demanded purposely—

"Say, mister, guess I didn't get you?"

"*Ach!*" said he quickly. "I ask your pardon! You are an American—I—"

"Don't let that worry you. Who in —— are you, and what're you doing up here anyway when a decent row's going on?"

He had sharp and small eyes, that guy, I noticed, as he gave Fieldmorre the once-over. I had another look at him. Small, wiry, fair, red tie, in a small cap and mean suit that looked like Whitechapel. I don't mean that the clothes made the man, but in this case the man seemed to have made the suit, if you get me. The sharp eyes darted from me to Fieldmorre, then to Billy, busy over by the door, and then to our bunch standing in a heap. He stroked his doll dog.

"I'm an old resident here and"—looking at Fieldmorre—"I thought you were off a Breetish man-o'-war."

"In mufti, no doubt," murmured Fieldmorre. "Well?"

"Nothing at all, sir. I am a student of life."

"Student of ——!" bawled one of our gang.

"Say, look here," interposed Billy, "we're going quietly home, but if you want trouble— You get me?"

Off came the little cap, and the owner replied—

"As you wish, sir; I but remark—"

His dog barked shrilly at that moment, producing a guffaw from our crowd.

"You remark too much, sir," retorted Billy. "Goodnight."

Fieldmorre smiled as he said, turning—

"Come on, you chaps."

As he went off in the hired launch for the *Penguin* I felt mighty easy. The drunken crowd were singing; but I knew that we were—well, knitted, I guess, is the best word.

By agreement Fieldmorre was skipper. My first thought had been, could he command a bunch such as ours were? I'd got my answer. I know I ain't great at taking orders from another, and our crowd wasn't used to it an' all that; but with Billy and Fieldy it differed a heap. When we got aboard that night I felt like a husband well mated—and I know what that means.

"Some bunch," as Billy remarked in the cuddy afterward.

"They are," agreed the old man, "and I wouldn't give a ——— for 'em if they weren't. That little Welshman—botanist or painter, isn't he?—and those two carroty-headed sons of—"

His blue eyes sparkled, and the fringe of his half-bald head twitched.

"Let's send 'em a double tot of rum and— Steward! What do you fellows think? And a bottle of dry fizz for the health—I'm superstitious, y'know— for the health of the ship?"

Sitting in the cuddy that night with the lamp burning under a skylight— while the sea danced a grave pavan—sure I've dabbled with music as well as women—outside the porthole—maybe I was drunk, but not with alcohol, but with love of a good ship and comrades.

But we hadn't seen the last of our friend sitting on the table. He turned up the very next morning while we were cussing because a lighter with the last tank of water had got adrift. He was more dolled up than before, I noticed, as he pranced up the gangway, and he'd left his little dog at home.

"Good morning," said he in the perfect accent of a foreigner.

"Good morning," said I as first mate.

"I wish to see the master."

"Right," said I, and led him to the cabin, where the skipper was playing chess with the supercargo—on paper.

"Yes," said Fieldmorre, looking up.

"*Bon jour, monseigneur.* If you permit me," continued the man, "I present myself, the Baron Bertouche."

"Speak English if you please," interrupted Fieldmorre politely.

"Certainly—or German or Italian or Spanish, if your lordship wishes," returned the stranger insolently.

Fieldmorre glanced at me. Billy was abstractedly shifting the chess-pieces about. There was an almost imperceptible smile on his face.

"D'you mind throwing the baron overboard?" Fieldy said quietly.

Billy looked up and grinned interestedly.

"Sure," said I, I fear with much feeling.

The baron's eyes became smallish. He looked at me stupidly as if to weigh me. I felt as if he'd asked me whether I could swim. I said—

"You'd better!"

He seemed to think so too; bowed, while Fieldmorre stared coldly and Billy grinned, and then followed me to the gangway.

At the creak of dawn we sailed for Accra.

VI

I HAD RATHER WONDERED AT FIELDMORRE'S HIGH-HANDED MANNER with the stranger at Las Palmas, but as he knew those waters and was skipper to boot, I naturally waited until an opportunity occurred to find out, which was one evening when we were watching Sirius just over the horizon from the poop.

"Oh, the baron's well known around here and Morocco," he replied, in answer to some odd reference, "where he's known among the people as *Sid el Keleeb*."

"The master of the little dog!" commented Billy. "Because of that mutt he carries around?"

"Yes. He carts that cur all over the shop; even used to have a kind of kennel for the brute rigged on his horse or camel. In northern Morocco he's finished, practically. Every blessed Arab knows him too well—to his cost—the Moors I mean. Even Bibi Starleton. I picked him up on my first trip here; found the bold bad baron in Funchal teaching languages.

"Perfectly true that he can speak German, Italian, Spanish, French, English, besides his own language, Danish. No doubt that's why I hired the blighter as an Arabic interpreter, possibly the only language he can't speak," added Fieldmorre, with his silent laugh.

"I'd chartered a small schooner, the *St. Paul*, loaded trade goods; and I took him with me. I called in at Mogador to look up a Moor whom I'd met on my road out for the latest information regarding Juby. Fortunately for me we stopped there a few days, at the end of which, my Moor gave me a tip and I shunted Master Baron thunderin' quick.

"It appeared that he'd been busy on board working up a nice little plot with some other cutthroats among the crew whom he knew, to slit my throat and heave me overboard on the trip, and then to pinch the cargo, scuttle the *St. Paul*—for they daren't have stuck to her in those waters—and skedaddle to pastures new, so to speak."

"He's got a cast-iron nerve to show up in Las Palmas then," I commented.

"Not he. He knew well enough I couldn't prove anything against him. And he'd nerve enough probably to think that he could blackmail me or something. How he lives now I don't know. Shouldn't be surprized if he's still in with Mannesman, the Hamburg people. They tried to get all the mining concessions in Morocco, you know."

Under the pretense of coastwise trading, we picked up our bunch of Hausa at various ports, all ex-soldiers. Fortunately, in these waters, official folk are mostly too sun and whisky soaked to be over-curious, so that we didn't bump trouble. We had fair weather for this time of the year, and within six weeks came slapping back under the trade winds.

The first sight you get of Juby is the spot of the old fort-factory, for the land beyond is as flat as the palm of your hand. Rather open for anchorage, but protected by a reef through which Fieldmorre—I believe he and one other are about the only humans who know the passage—conned us prettily. As we dropped anchor, a noticeable bustle was remarked on the beach in front of the small village, and on the fort fluttered a Union Jack.

The three of us went ashore, Fieldmorre, Billy and I. We found Hardwicke and Broughton and Sabah, but Vèron had not turned up, although we were already some ten days overdue.

This seemed strange, as we had had a wire at Las Palmas, dating his departure from Mogador, and since then he had had more than enough time to reach Juby overland.

However, there was nothing to be done. Hardwicke and Broughton had, mainly with Sabah's assistance, done excellently well in getting beasts. But Sabah, according to Billy and Fieldmorre, had altered, seemingly mighty depressed that he hadn't been able to scout any information worth having all the time he had been around Ma-el-Einen, from whom he had brought presents and pretty phrases which at any rate sounded well.

Anyway we got busy discharging and humping the cargo on to the beach—some long and tiresome job with only the ship's boats and the few native punts we could scare up. Our fellows, even the orthodox crew, no doubt wondered what in the name of Heaven these savages wanted with agricultural machinery and pianos, for none of these cases were opened until the *Penguin* had put to sea.

Everything had gone like clockwork. The Hausa, hungry for any excuse— all worked up at the promise of blood and imaginary loot—drilled and practised at improvised rifle-butts like sons of guns; and our fellows were just fine—none quicker on the jump than Fieldmorre's two compatriots, Casey and O'Donnell. Although we expected Vèron any day, he did not show up.

Knowing well that the news of the landing would have spread up-country and be discussed in the bazaars of towns, we hurried things, but it was ten days later—no doubt to the astonishment of Allah's local followers—when, on October 26th, the column took the trail, two hundred and fifty strong, including servants and camp-followers.

Naturally, coming to clear grips with the real thing, we talked our heads off, discussing the pros and cons of the venture over the camp-fire at night, and read and reread every word of Thorpe's tragic diary. Another point of more immediate concern was Ma-el-Einen's reception. If he should choose to get fresh at the sight of our little army, we'd have a fight on our hands right there or before. Sabah still appeared, if not sullen, sulky about something; and his manner seemed hard to fit in with the theory of disappointment; yet the man himself I rather cottoned to.

However, we jogged along day after day with never a sight of a possible enemy. Not even the nomad Tuareg who had hustled Billy and Fieldmorre on their first trip broke the monotony.

Old man Ma-el-Einen's hang-out was a walled town, almost a village, perched on the only bit of a hill in the country, close to a *donga*, as we call 'em down south; that is, a dry course—dry, except by digging—for eleven months out of the year and then it gets wet only thanks to the melting of the snows on the distant Atlas Mountains. From his attitude when he received the three of us you would have thought we and our crazy expedition were no more to him than some old camel-driver limping in on the Sudan trail.

He accepted presents and returned—some—and listened to our demands for assistance in the shape of fodder and water with the same "I'm-in-heaven-chinning-with-the-Prophet-run-away-and don't-bother" expression of a *pukka* saint.

Naturally we tried all we knew to get some information out of the old man or his boys, but, just as Billy had complained, they either ignored the questions or swore by Allah and the Prophet they had never heard of any such country. You couldn't give 'em the lie, as it was feasible that they, being interested only in the Sudan trail, which passed a long way to the north of our goal, and not being curious folk, didn't know or care a fig what tribes, except for raiding, were below them. Seemed queer, though, all the same.

While we were resting over a few days a holy man—dervish kind of guy—wandered into the town. We struck him first when we were coming back from the last interview with the old boy, who got quite affable—if you could imagine a stone Buddha affable—and sent extra presents after us with special recommendations to the care of Allah.

He—the dervish, not the pope—was busy shouting and foaming at the mouth and mussing around with a bunch of snakes before a solemn crowd. As we pulled up to rubber he screamed louder than ever, and, catching one snake, rammed it into his mouth and appeared to swallow it, darned near making me sick on the spot.

This same crazy guy turned up in camp and did similar stunts, much to the admiration of our Hausa, who, native-like, thought he was great stuff as a holy man. When we struck camp a few days later, Billy Sunday, as our Billy had irreverently nicknamed him, took it into his holy nut to come along too. For reasons of native policy, as Fieldmorre put it, we didn't hoof him out. Anyway, except for raising fanatical mania—as I knew his kidney among the Mahdi—he seemed a harmless loony.

Fieldmorre and Billy were still considerably worried that Vèron had not turned up. Had he been unable to come by reason of sickness, he could have sent a messenger. They began to fear that he'd struck trouble on the road, but without details we couldn't attempt anything.

After Ma-el-Einen's village the going was fierce; not so much for us on dromedaries but for the Hausa, who were unused to the ankle-gripping sand of the Sahara. The fifth night out we struck a better trail, left the desert proper and found a bare and rocky plateau.

That night, as we were sitting round the fire of camel or dromedary dung, the headman of the pack-team came up and jabbered away with Sabah in Shilhah. Sabah, looking more dismal than ever, reported that five dromedaries were sick with a sickness that they did not know.

This seemed rotten luck. We went across and had a look at them, and they surely looked down and out, three of them crouched camel fashion with their heads on the sand. None of us knew anything about the dromedary—the only thing we could do was to cuss and pray. All five were dead the following morning; and on the top of that, seven men turned up complaining of pains in their tummies. The loads were spread over the other pack-animals, and we got under way a little late.

During the march that day the seven sick men became worse, and at the midday halt Seeger reported that each had a high temperature, but he couldn't satisfactorily diagnose the trouble—an acute diarrhea, yet he was sure that it wasn't dysentery. That night three more dromedaries and five more men were on the sick list. Eight beasts put out of mess began to complicate the transport. We held a powwow, but couldn't arrive at any solution, either as to a remedy or as to the cause of the trouble, and the misfortune began to make us a bit down in the mouth.

The next day two men died; four more and three animals went sick. Sabah looked like a half-plucked sick hen. Next morning, as we delayed to let their comrades bury them, two others pegged out, which held us up for the day.

Also I noticed that our Hausa, real fine fellows ordinarily but as subject to superstition as most, were beginning to mutter among themselves.

"Glory," thought I, "if they get a bug in their heads that we're bewitched, then there'll be the —— to pay."

Billy and Fieldmorre knew this as well as I did, but we didn't say anything. In three days we lost another seven dromedaries, had eleven men dead and fourteen sick on our hands. Queer part was that none of the usual remedies seemed to have any effect; forty drops of laudanum only deadened the pain somewhat.

The look of the Hausa I didn't like at all; even the loony holy man had quit snake-swallowing and sat fakir fashion 'most all the time in camp, regarding Allah or somebody. I had kept my eye on that guy, too, watching out for any attempt at stirring them up against the infidel.

That night we talked long and seriously. We almost prayed in a way for a happy band of Tuareg to come and pay a visit, just to cheer up the Hausa and distract their attention. But around this forsaken district never a moving thing was seen save away up sometimes a prowling vulture or a stray eagle from the Atlas. The country ahead looked like petering out into sheer sand again, so that night we filled all the water-skins—not as many as we had had, for lack of transport.

The following afternoon, as we were swaying along, I suddenly felt dizzy; came over like a wave and passed. About an hour afterward I got it again, accompanied by a cold sweat, with a gripping pain which doubled me up.

"Oh, my ——," thought I, "it's got me."

But it passed again. Fieldmorre, who was riding close beside me, I saw suddenly bite his lip and crouch slightly.

"Say, are you feeling bad, skipper?" I called out.

He straightened up.

"Oh, nothing at all," he replied with a smile.

I urged my beast up alongside him.

"You look mighty white about the gills anyway," I continued.

"So do you," he retorted, grinning, "heat probably. This sun's infernal. You know," he went on, "I've been looking up that French map and I half think we ought to bear a couple of points more to the southward to strike the wells which are supposed to be there."

"You're navigating officer," I replied, "so I guess it's up to you."

"Well, William agrees, so I suppose we'd better shift—"

Another spasm took him and myself at the same moment.

"We've both got it, I guess," I said when we had recovered.

"I'm afraid so," he admitted, grimacing, and hailed the nearest man, who happened to be Casey, to shout for the doc. We loaded up then and there with laudanum, enough to get to camp without rolling off our beasts—and even

THE LAND OF OPHIR

then that was some —— trip.

That night I admit I didn't know anything about the expedition, nor did I care. I seemed to be able to keep enough head on me to swear and insist that I wouldn't cash in, for sometimes I surely felt like it.

One day I was Phil Tromp once more and could sit up and take notice. At first I couldn't make out what the heaving glare of white light could be; then I figured out the sand and began to wonder where I was. Finally I discovered that I was mewed up in a kind of wicker basket slung on the side of my dromedary.

I lay—or was huddled—a long time squaring things, kind of getting my bearings in this world again. I tried to sit up, and found out how darned weak I was. Presently I saw Billy's face come swimming out of heaven.

"Fine!" said I. "How's Fieldmorre?"

"Just about as fine as you are, old boy," returned Billy dryly. "You've both had a rough passage, believe me."

"Oh, sure I do!" I assured him.

Billy grinned.

"That's the whichaway!"

I peeked out of my trap at the caravan sprawling over the sands.

"Lordy!" I exclaimed. "Is that Vèron over there?"

"Sure it's Vèron. He overtook us about a week ago."

"A—a week?"

"Yes; you've been bad about ten days. Vèron overtook us, and then we began to see things."

"What do you mean?"

"That crazy Billy Sunday guy's been poisoning the animals and men ever since he joined us at Ma-el-Einen's, and even sticking holes in the water-skins. Vèron was captured by Tuareg, with a caravan he was traveling with, and this guy gave him away as a Christian. They started in to fix him; but Vèron—he's some boy!—stole one of their fastest camels and made a bee-line to cut our trail, which he did."

"And the dervish guy?"

"Shot—*pronto*."

VII

I GUESS I WAS SICKER THAN I THOUGHT, for I didn't realize for a few days that Billy was treating both Fieldmorre and me as convalescents; kind of slops and quiet, don't let him talk too much, nurse. Most of the time I slept, either in my wicker cage or in camp—so did Fieldmorre—the why of our comparative rapid recovery I reckoned. Then I got wise to the fact that something was wrong by a chance conversation overheard between Hibbert and Famitty.

"Don't like it at all, I don't," the former remarked. "What the —— did the old man let that marabout* blighter come along for? Might ha' known."

"Guess he knows what he's doin'," insisted Famitty loyally. "These Mohammedan guys get mighty sore if you muss about with their holy guys."

"Go on," retorted Hibbert; "I know 'em. I ain't spent ten years on the Somali coast for nothing. Don't like this 'ere Frenchie either, if you ask me. He's too 'igh and mighty for me. Thinks he knows everything."

"Aw, cut it out," growled Famitty. "You don't get a word he says anyway. But he sure knows these Hausa fellows and the country around these parts. The only thing that keeps me guessing is about the shooting of that snake-swallower. Don't do to try fool stunts with these guys."

"That's what I'm gettin' at!" snapped Hibbert. "Ought to have shoved him out into the desert and let him chase 'isself, that's what I say."

They went on arguing, but what they had already said had made me sit up. Not the attitude of criticism; for, knowing men more or less, I was sure that whatever they thought, either man would stick right through if any real trouble began. But Hibbert had dangerous makings, being, as there is in almost any crew, a kind of sea-lawyer.

However, that woke me up to the fact that the holy man had started something, corroborated soon by the remarks of a couple of our Hausa who were quarreling—about what I didn't get, but evidently to do with this darned dervish. The Hausa, I knew, are about forty per cent Mohammedan, forty per cent pagan and the rest nothing in particular, but all doped with superstition, magic witchcraft, and the like.

That night, probably because I was stirred up, I noticed a certain kind of awkwardness, or thought I did, around the fire; and I got a bit riled— foolishly I knew—because Fieldmorre was evidently pressed into service to translate for Billy and Vèron. I didn't realize until some time afterward what a nasty mess Billy must have been in. As he couldn't speak French he had to fall back on Arabic to talk with Vèron or otherwise use Sabah as interpreter. I wasn't happy at all that night when I turned in; for the most dangerous thing that could happen on such an expedition was dissension in any form by misunderstanding or fool jealousy.

Next day we were passing through a forsaken piece of country of scrub and sand and shale, more desolate than the real desert. I rode alongside Billy and asked him, bluffing gaiety, what was the trouble. At first he shied. I spoke straight.

"Say here, Billy, cut out the nursie business. Maybe I'm not fit yet in my body, but my think-tank's working overtime. Something's wrong. What is it?"

---

* A Mohammedan holy man.

"That's right, Phil, there is; but I don't quite know what's the matter. The best thing that I could think up was for you—and Fieldmorre—to get fit, but while you were sick, filling you up with trouble wouldn't help you any."

"What is the trouble? Vèron?"

"No. That darned dervish. You remember when we decided to let him come along to keep our native bunch quiet. We all agreed on that. 'Smatter of fact, the only thing I was scared of was that he might start religious trouble."

"Same here," said I.

"But I never reckoned on the poisoning stunt. For one reason I couldn't find a motive, and I'm darned if I can now."

"Except natural religious prejudice. Probably, he betrayed Vèron out of similar cussedness."

"Uh! Uh! Mighty awkward, Vèron showing up when you two went sick. Don't know a darn word of French—not enough to talk—and—"

"I know. But get to the meat."

"The point is that there's some trouble among the Hausa. Vèron knows it, too. He reckons, according to Fieldy, that it's just the usual squabble between the Mohammedans and the pagans. But I doubt it. I've got a hunch that darned snake-swallowing swine put some bug in their heads purposely."

I agreed, although I didn't hammer on the fact. I shifted over later and had a chat with Fieldmorre. He was much to my way of thinking. That evening we talked out around the fire. We decided to keep the various factions apart as much as possible by dividing them into watches. There was no open sedition, but just the simmer of discontent resulting in sudden flurries of disputes, the Mohammedans inclining to spit at the others and they becoming naturally resentful. But the point I chewed on was: If the dervish had started this—for what purpose?

According to the skipper we were due for another stretch of waterless desert, and then we ought to strike the northern spur of the desolate hills mentioned in Thorpe's diary. The next day Hardwicke gave me something more to think about. Riding alongside on the road, he began vaguely talking about things in general when suddenly he came out with—

"D'you know, I wish we hadn't got Vèron in the party."

"Why?"

"Oh, I don't know. There seems something ruddy queer to me sometimes. What was he doing up beyond so long? Can't quite swallow that yarn about being captured and all that."

"Don't talk bull!" I snapped. "What the blazes d'you think? Didn't he spot that dervish guy and—"

"Yes, I know, but—"

"But what?"

"Well, he's a captain in the French army and it doesn't seem reasonable to me that he's going to help us to pinch this empire for England."

"We're not going to pinch it for England," I retorted, rather riled.

"Oh, yes, we are. The company's English, and anyway we're bound to have a political standing. Officially I mean. We can't stand alone. The Rhodesian or the Niger or the old John Company of India, they're British. Doesn't seem reasonable to me that a Frenchman's going to stand for that. He's either not playing the game to us or to his country."

"By ——, you've started something!" I exclaimed, for I admit that point of view had not struck me. "But why in —— didn't you spit it out before?"

"How could I? Wasn't he in with Fieldmorre and Langster before we came?"

That was true, but I felt mad.

"If you're thinking that way," I snapped, "go and tell Fieldmorre. He's skipper."

"All right," retorted Hardwicke in his English way; "don't get your hair off."

I was mad; not with Hardwicke, but at the evident threat of a split among the white leaders as well. And what got me real worried was the fact that Hardwicke's point of view didn't seem unreasonable. After all, thinking it over, I had just taken for granted that Vèron was O.K. merely because he was in with Billy. Still I felt mighty sore and thoughtful that night as I lay staring at the stars and listening to the grumbling of the dromedaries.

This sort of thing gets on your nerves. Maybe I was still sicker than I knew; anyway I began to feel a morose resentment against everybody, and, worse, found myself watching odd people suspiciously and wondering what was going on inside their nuts.

I even started to work up a resentment against Fieldmorre. We'd agreed that he was to be in command, and I was loyal right through; but childishly I began to complain to myself, asking why the blazes didn't he pull everybody together. Then I recollected that I wasn't fair, for both of us had been knocked out of the running for a fortnight, nigh. As I nevertheless was gloomily regarding Sabah drooping over the hump of his animal like a mangy buzzard on a fence, Fieldmorre came alongside.

"Feeling fit, Tromp?" he demanded, and the brisk sound of his voice bucked me up.

"Pretty nigh," I replied.

"Good."

His blue eyes regarded me swiftly.

"William!" he hailed Billy, who was riding a few yards away. "Look here, you fellows," he continued when Billy had joined us, "we've got to pull this crowd together. I don't know whether you'll agree with me, but there's too much idle chatter about."

"That's right," concurred Billy.

"Tromp and I have both been in sick bay, and you, William—forgive my putting it like this—have been rather hobbled by lack of French."

"Lordy, don't I know it!" agreed Billy.

"You chaps have agreed that I'm to be skipper, so it's my job to speak out. Are you with me? Well—you forgive me, Tromp? I know William, because we've been up here before. Frankly, things look —— rotten. As far as we three are concerned—well, we'll play cricket. Of course that's understood. There's a sort of dry rot among us. See?

"Look at Sabah there. Looks like a ruddy sick camel—and other little things. The men have got a touch of it too. Well, we've got to set the pace. I hope you chaps understand?"

"Sure we do."

"Oh, that's all I wanted to say."

Billy and I looked at each other, both wondering at a Celt being as inarticulate as an Anglo-Saxon. Yet we were both Anglo-Saxons!

"Why did you speak of Sabah, Fieldy?" queried Billy after a moment's silence. "Don't you think he's straight?"

"As far as I know," returned Fieldmorre, "but one must remember, once a Mohammedan always a Mohammedan."

"What d'you mean?" I demanded, thinking, "Oh, Lordy, here's another of 'em!"

"Oh, only that—er—when you're driven down to basic—er—elemental principles, that a Christian's a Christian and a Mohammedan's a Mohammedan."

"Lordy!" thought I. "Why is a piece of string? Because it isn't. Yet—"

However, I got what he meant; but the idea didn't cheer me any. Later, when Billy and I happened to be together, he grinned understandingly. Somehow we both felt better. About an hour later, in the afternoon, when we were looking for a camp site, one of our flankers, Sarkard, came scurrying in with the report that he'd seen a solitary mounted man on the horizon.

"Double the sentries tonight," was Fieldmorre's comment.

However, nothing happened; nor did our folk locate a sign of a living thing for two more days. When we had arrived in sight of the gneiss hills, it came with the rising of the sun as we were in the middle of striking camp.

A picket to the south, posted on a rump of a small hill, suddenly shattered the desert's stillness with the familiar *rat-tat-a-tat* of a Maxim.

"Posts!" shouted Fieldmorre, who was waiting for his beast to kneel, and I swear there was an exultant note in his voice.

"Posts!" shouted Barnard, echoing the tone. "Come along, you fellows. Form square. Recall!" he bellowed as against the scarlet light of the rising sun appeared a shadow of galloping horsemen.

The trumpet of a Hausa squalled harshly.

"Thank the good Lord," I thought as I yelled at my men, who, Mohammedan and pagan, showed not the slightest sign of hesitation. Even the dromedary drivers and camp-followers ran to drive their beasts into the center of the square as they had been drilled.

Casey, with his inseparable half-section, O'Donnell bringing his picket on the run as recalled, yelled exultantly—

"By gob, there's millions of the darlin's, Lord bless 'em!"

Somewhere I heard our botanist-painter screaming—

"Indeed to goodness, if you don't get that ruddy camel out of the way I'll—"

Casey's report was somewhat exaggerated but they certainly came on like locusts, as the prophet might say. Vèron, with his bunch of Hausa, was the first to get in action, as all had orders to reserve their fire until within killing distance. They came from every side at once, in the typical Arab style, yelling like loonies and firing from the saddle. Some of their bullets got home.

One of my men grunted and collapsed. I heard another scream, and a dromedary roared, but mostly they spurted sand before us or sang over our heads.

One or two overexcited men popped several erratic shots into them as they rode —— for leather, but the others held their fire, rifle and machine-gun, until they were seemingly almost on top of us. Then Vèron opened the ball, and from the four sides came the rattle of the Maxim and crash of volleys.

Standing beside my machine section, with an eye on it in case she jammed, I thought for one moment that they would sweep right over us. They seemed as thick as bees.

Riders, with the long black locks sticking out above their veils, shot off their animals as they plunged, dropped, or swerved madly. The second and third volleys, even with the machine going for all she was worth, failed to bring 'em up. A bullet whined past my head as, drawing my revolver, I began emptying into the ruck of the glaring eyes and gleaming lances, not more than ten yards distant away. Their yells sounded above the clatter of the guns. Although in some confusion from maddened animals, they came right on top of us through a hell of lead. I heard Fieldmorre shouting:

"Bayonet! Bayonet!" echoed by Casey's bull voice on my left.

For several moments everything was just a general mix-up—shouts, yells, screams of animals amid the spluttering and rattling of the guns. A big bony devil, eyes glaring above his linen mask, appeared right on top of me as I was turning from another, slashed with his five-foot sword and missed.

I caught him by a bare ankle and heaved him off on to the bayonet of a big Hausa sergeant grinning like a fiend. Then, grabbing a handy bayonet, I waded in on my own, for these guys were own brothers to my Mahdi friends, and I had quite a few scores to pay off.

All the same I had to keep an eye on my own men. I stepped back a pace to see what they were up to—fighting like furies. Anyway the rush had been stopped and the square wasn't broken.

I guessed it was about time to charge and throw 'em off. I turned. Fieldmorre was standing on a bale of goods with his pipe in his mouth. I caught his eye and pantomimed drawing a sword to charge. He nodded, and, taking the pipe from his mouth, bawled orders generally.

But our offensive came almost too late, for after the failure of their first rush they tucked up and began scuttling for cover, so that the charge degenerated into a chase.

The only difficulty I had with my men was to get 'em back, for obviously if the Tuareg lured us far out of formation, rallied and charged again, they'd take us on the hip. However, they didn't, and amid much shouting and a few desultory shots they rode mighty hard to get out of rifle-range.

We had bagged quite a few wounded and killed. The trouble was what to do with the former. For information they were useless, for you could have cut 'em to pieces and never dug out a single word except hearty curses.

We had lost three killed and eleven wounded among the Hausa. Sarkard had gone—received a slug in the left temple; Barnard, Famitty and O'Donnell had sword and lance flesh-wounds.

We stuck to our camp for that day, but beyond racing about Arab fashion almost on the horizon, the Tuareg did not reattack. The most astonishing thing was the number of 'em—over a thousand at least, we estimated. And, as Vèron said, these nomads seldom travel in bunches of even a few hundred.

But all hands felt good that night. I did—although I was done in, for I hadn't yet got my strength back. The scrap had apparently healed all personal troubles. But the trials which the expedition was to suffer were merely beginning.

TO BE CONTINUED

THE LAND of OPHIR

A THREE-PART STORY
PART II

by
CHARLES BEADLE

The first part of the story briefly retold in story form.

ABOUT THE FIRST ADVENTURE I CAN REMEMBER was with Fraser H. Thorpe, back in early schooldays. It lasted sixteen rounds, and left me with a feeling of permanent disgrace—because I'd thought of Frazer as a sissy, a student, a bug-chaser, and not good for anything except hunting beetles. And that shows how wrong a man can be!

My name's Tromp, by the way.

What he did in the world I don't know. My luck took me with other men. And the prince of them was Billy Langster, one of the wildest who ever hit the Barbary Coast. But Billy disappeared—to become respectable, I understood; while I found myself trekking through the big thirsts in Africa with an Africander named Ollendorf.

We wandered all over the shop from Bulawayo to the Nile, where old Ollendorf kicked in—or, rather, was gored out by a buffalo. The last I recall of Ollendorf was when we ran into the *safari* of a Levantine who called himself Gandy, somewhere northwest of Lake Albert Edward. Gandy was beating up a woman with a *sjambok*; so we beat him up instead—and left him cursing us in languages we couldn't recognize and could treat with contempt.

The Mahdi got me shortly after this and kept me in a cage for a couple of years, dangling from dromedaries' backs in the eastern Sudan.

When I got free I settled down—and, to make quite sure, I got married.

Fate dealt me another hand a few years later, when I found myself a widower, alone, smoking a pipe in the lobby of a New York hotel. One night I went down into the old Tenderloin looking for some excitement with Hardwicke, a young Englishman I'd picked up in Mexico. And we found it. When the fight was over, Hardwicke—between drink and gratitude—spilled the beans about an expedition that was on foot for Africa.

Right away I horned in, and he introduced me to the leader. I took one look and recognized him.

"Billy!"

So old Billy Langster gave me the dope first hand.

He'd been about everywhere! New York, East Africa—where he was very nearly scuppered by a gang who first worshipped him and then wanted to eat him—China, Peru, Brazil, and Africa again—Morocco, to be exact, where he tried his hand at making sultans.

This sultan business naturally brought him up with fat Johnny Starleton. Every one knows Starleton—he really *does* make sultans! Through Starleton, Billy met another regular fellow, Fieldmorre, an impecunious Irish viscount, who had a hunch of his own.

Between them they'd got hold of Sabah, a Syrian who had gone in with a syndicate some years before to exploit the territory back of Juby, just south of the Spanish line on the West Coast where the Sûs ends in the sea.

The syndicate had gone on the bum when an assistant funked his job, and the local sheik was made to pay damages by a British gunboat. But there were rich pickings there; and Fieldmorre took up where the old syndicate ended.

With Sabah he went inland and visited the Shareef Ma-el-Einen, ruler of the entire district. They made friends with the *shareef* and a Frenchman, Captain Vèron, who butted in while on an exploring-trip from Senegal.

Vèron warned them it was sure death to go farther inland; told of atrocities— missing men—and so forth. The latest relic was the journal of a man who had gone in and not come out. Vèron had got the book from a coast Fantee.

Well, when Billy gave me that line, I grinned.

"All right, you —— cynic," said he; and he produced the diary.

This diary-writing adventurer gave a pretty straight account of hitting inland to Nsonnafo's village; and from there on until he struck a city of "oriental magnificence" and met the sultan. Then he began to gibber about subphratries of the Snake Society—and sacrifices—and that was all. The account ended right there. It was —— interesting, but not conclusive. I turned the book over in my hand—and a name almost slapped me in the face:

FRASER HALDE THORPE

I told Billy, without any more palaver, that I was good for $20,000 for my share in the expedition. Where Frazy had gone I'd go!

We recruited our whites from men we'd known, and arranged for them to meet us at Funchal and Las Palmas, where we picked them up some months later on our own schooner, *Penguin*, and sailed for Juby.

But in Las Palmas we had a farewell rough-house when our men got in a row that brought us the acquaintance of Baron Bertouche—known to the masses as Sid-el-Keleeb, a man who sponged on the whole world until he met Fieldmorre, who came near kicking him overboard.

Well, when we reached Juby we found all hands present, except Vèron, who sent a message that he would overtake us.

Ten days later then, two hundred and fifty strong—one hundred of these being fighting Hausas trained by ourselves at the butts with rifle and machine gun—we hit the long trail.

We found Ma-el-Einen all right, polite enough in his walled town, but kind of sore at us going any farther. Sabah, too, suddenly began to balk and get sullen for no reason we could see. And we got our first taste of the real desert when we picked up a dervish—a dirty, snake-swallowing, shrieking, blasphemous dervish—who gave our Hausas (half of 'em were Mohammedans; half were rank pagan) a real thrill.

After we'd gone about five days' march into the desert sickness began to break out. First it hit the dromedaries. Then the men caught it. When they began to cash in, the Hausas showed signs of funk. We couldn't figure it out. One day as I was talking it over with Fieldmorre a spasm took him and myself at the same moment.

"Fieldy," said I, "we've both got it."

We loaded up immediately with laudanum; and the next thing I remembered—Oh, ——, I don't remember anything.

We came to ten days later in wicker baskets slung from dromedaries.

The caravan was still intact.

Vèron had succeeded in joining us, after escaping from Tuaregs. If he hadn't joined us, —— knows what would have happened. He caught on right away that the dervish had been slowly poisoning the whole outfit, and punching holes in the water-skins.

"What ——" I began.

"Shot 'm—*pronto*," says Billy.

But that didn't seem to settle things either, because he had put the fear of —— into the lot of the men. The morale was kind of shaken. Irritation and complaining began to break out. We all got the infection.

Some of us believed Vèron was double-crossing us in the interests of France; others thought Sabah's actions suspicious; and an undercurrent of resentment was soon threatening to disrupt us. Only one thing could have saved us. And it happened.

Camp was jumped at dawn by a whirlwind of Tuaregs.

We fell back into square and gave 'em ——, beating them off after a good sharp scrap.

We knew now our Hausas could fight!

But we knew, too—and every passing hour confirmed it—that the unknown reaches before us held unguessed dangers and swarmed with terrible fighters.

And I couldn't forget the Mahdi!

VIII

IN THE MORNING THERE WAS NO SIGN OF THE TUAREG. We hit the trail as early as possible, we whites taking it in turn to walk, as the wounded required some of the dromedaries.

Naturally, going through the district where Thorpe had had such a bad time, his diary occupied much of our attention. Although he had approached from the Senegal side, that is from the southwest, and we were coming in from practically due west, there was no doubt, to judge by the formation, that these hills were the same. Profiting by his experience, we had filled up every water-skin we could carry and placed every one on half-rations.

By a kind of mutual consent, each feeling that the action had wounded any rifts there might be—at any rate among the Hausa—we did not mention the subject of any possible dissension, although I guessed there was pretty hard thinking going on. I for one couldn't forget Hardwicke's point of view regarding Vèron, and utterly failed to reconcile a French officer being in on such a filibustering outfit. Of course it might be so. And Sabah, too—who had had a finger chopped off, which didn't seem to please him any—seemed as sulky as before.

The most cheering thing I noticed was that our Hausa appeared in excellent spirits, jabbering their heads off, each man in his fashion relating the prodigies he had performed. The heat, hit up by the refraction from the rocks as Thorpe had mentioned, surely was fierce. Seeger, the doc, was kept pretty busy with his wounded, although none of them, except two Hausa who died the following day, had been very seriously injured.

Naturally we kept double sentries out, prepared for any attack at any time, but the Tuareg seemed to have quit for good. I remarked that Fieldmorre was doing a lot of chin-wagging with Vèron, and purposely left them alone.

The more I tried to figure things out, the more balled up I got; for it seemed, on further reflection, that had he been a French spy he, knowing from the beginning what was on the cards, would have had a French war-ship or British—as the two were in accord at the moment over the Morocco and allied questions—at Juby to chase us off. I decided that Hardwicke was talking bunk and tried to dismiss the subject from my mind.

Dromedaries just hate marching on stone as much as a cat hates walking in the rain, and they showed signs of getting sore feet. We reckoned that we were traveling faster than Thorpe had been able to do, for he had had porters heavily laden. Two days later I began, as Thorpe had done, watching those infernal hills as he had called them, and wondering when they were going to end.

Our scouts found no sign nor sight of any of our late friends, and we were disposed to think that, in spite of their unusual numbers, they must have been an extra big gang just after loot in the customary way. The following afternoon, toward sunset, the hills began to peter out and we saw ahead the plateau of shale and sand which had pretty nigh done for Thorpe.

Late that night—that is, for camp-life—as we were sitting around the fire discussing matters, my ears, which are pretty acute, caught a queer sound. At first I thought I was imagining things.

"D'you hear that, you fellows?" I asked.

We all listened intently. Faintly but distinctly came a distant cry sounding half-human. We all had heard it. The night was starry but dark. Again it came and seemed chopped off. This time we located the direction unanimously.

"Who's in charge of the picket to the west?" inquired Fieldmorre.

"Pexton," said I, and hailed him. "D'you hear that cry out in the desert?" I asked.

He listened. After a moment it came again.

"Indeed I do," he replied. "What would you be thinking it is?"

"That's what we're wondering. Say, just go out and see if your fellows have spotted anything."

"Half a second," said Billy. "I'm orderly officer tonight. May as well do the rounds now. Come along."

The pair padded off into the night and we sat listening for the recurrence of the strange cry, which happened several times.

"*C'est un être humain*," exclaimed Vèron with conviction.

"Certainly doesn't sound like a jackal, and I can't for the life of me think what else it could be," commented Fieldmorre.

Presently we heard Billy's and Pexton's voices on the still hot air. Then we saw the flash of a torch and dun figures making their way across the open. For some time the cry was not repeated. At last it came again, just as the distant light had been smothered by a rise in the sandy soil and shale.

At length into the light about us stalked Pexton and Billy, and behind them a big Hausa carrying on his shoulders what seemed at first sight to be the corpse of our late friend the marabout.

"What is it?" demanded Fieldmorre.

"Dunno," replied Billy. "Seems crazy or dying. Don't know which."

The Hausa dumped the man by the side of the fire. He was an elderly native with a white beard and mustache, not negroid, but rather the Fulani-Berber type. His robe was old and patched and moreover nearly in rags. He moaned loudly as he lay in a crumpled heap, and we recognized the mysterious cry from the desert.

We called Seeger. He thought that the fellow seemed pegging out from exhaustion. His body was badly nourished, as the newspapers say.

"Give him a shot of something to pull him together," suggested Billy. "Perhaps he'll be able to talk."

At the prick of the needle the old man started visibly, but his eyes didn't open. Seeger bent down and lifted his lids and flashed a torch.

"The son of a gun's playing 'possum, I believe," he said.

"Give him a swig of whisky," suggested Barnard. "That'll bring him back from ——."

Barnard was more or less right, for the old guy spluttered at the first taste and then spat it out vigorously, raising a laugh from us all. He sat up after that. I guess the doc's dope began to work too. For his eyes looked good and bright as he stared around at the group of whites. Probably he'd never seen so many in all his life.

Vèron butted in and began talking. He replied in a dialect of Arabic, thanking Allah for his merciful rescue with variations.

"Who art thou and whence comest thou, O my father?" interrupted Fieldmorre, taking the lead. The old fellow blinked at the circle of watching eyes.

"Who are ye?" he retorted to the speaker. "And what do ye here in the land of thirst?"

"Blast his cheek!" muttered Barnard.

"We travel from the west into the east, O my father," replied Fieldmorre quietly. "How earnest thou in this sorry plight?"

"I was traveling from the tents of the Ibn Badwahi to the Fahamwata, when my camel was stricken and died. My feet are old and feeble, and I fell by the wayside. But Allah is All Merciful, Knowing, Compassionate, Wise!"

"Where are the bones of thy beast?" butted in Vèron again.

"Nigh unto five days' marching for an old man, to the south."

"Are there wells nigh to here, O my father?" queried Fieldmorre.

"To the north, for seven swift days; to the east none for ten fast days," replied the old man.

"Glory!" I murmured. "Ten days!"

And I hoped to —— he was lying.

"Give me to rest, O white man, for I am feeble."

"You'd better look after him, doc," said Fieldmorre. "He certainly looks bad."

They carried him off to the Hausa quarters, and Seeger went to look after him. The remainder of us tried to figure out who and what he was. His yarn seemed plausible enough to me, and Fieldmorre and Billy agreed. But Vèron wouldn't have it; nor Barnard. The former jabbered away to Fieldmorre, venting strong views on the subject which made me think—

"The fellow can't be a French traitor, otherwise he'd be only too darned glad to see the expedition wiped out, as long as he got away."

I always keep my eyes skinned, so that during the next day's march I didn't fail to notice several things: Seeger cussing, but quite harmlessly, at having another patient wished on to him, when, as it was, the transport was overtaxed; Hibbert and Famitty arguing again, the former insisting that we ought to have shot this blighter as we had the other; and among the Hausa was a distinct return to the factional disputes between Mohammedans and pagans.

Sabah, if it were possible, seemed more depressed than ever. I tried to talk to him, but all I could get were monosyllables and a dreary statement that he was sick.

"How?" said I; but he wouldn't or couldn't explain.

As we trudged on in silence—for I was doing my spell on the road—he remarked plaintively that he'd known Fieldmorre for ten years.

"What's the trouble about that?" I demanded. "Nothing to grumble for, is there?"

He mumbled something unintelligible and refused to explain.

"Maybe he's sickening up for something," thought I, and wandered off into vague speculations as to what kind of guy the sultan of these people whom we were out to get would turn out to be. Surely a fanatical Mohammedan; probably Berber or Fulani.

Next morning, as we were drinking our allowance of coffee and at the moment talking vaguely about how long Thorpe's desert, as we had named it, would last, there came a sudden rifle-shot. As we sprang for our guns, yelling orders to the men, there followed an outburst of erratic rifle-fire, far too much for any single picket. As we looked we saw the sun-gleams of the lances of a bunch of horsemen sweep up and right over the forms of the picket. Looking to the west, I beheld another party riding like the —— past the picket. As I was wondering why they did not fire, the truth struck me. Hardwicke, standing near me, had seen it and bawled out—

"By ——, we're betrayed!"

"Shut your head," I shouted angrily, knowing that that was the quickest road to start a panic.

"Each man take a machine," yelled Fieldmorre, for we had all seen it, "and shoot the first man who tries to bolt."

Again Vèron was one of the first on the job—Lordy, he was some soldier! The sergeant in charge of his section was a Mohammedan and had the Maxim already mounted; he tried deliberately to swing it upon us. Vèron shot him, and, seizing the gun, opened her on the bunch drawing down on us.

Meanwhile Fieldmorre, Billy and I and the others—the boys were mighty quick to tumble—ran to the guns, shooting when necessary. Sudden scraps started up between our own people.

Several of the drivers attempted to turn the beasts loose. Five got away, trailing across the desert, three of them with wounded, yelling and sticking their heads from their baskets.

My bunch fortunately remained loyal, so that while the sergeant was busy with the Maxim, I was free to look at other things. I had a vision of Casey slashing right and left with a rifle-butt on the men who had turned upon him, and on the other side our painter-botanist using two guns. Hardwicke's section I saw was sticking; and, shouting to him to help Casey, I ran to Pexton's assistance.

In the middle of the scrap, just as we had got some of them under—many quit cold and bolted—and I was busy with two of 'em, the charging bunch hit us. I don't know—nor does Billy nor Fieldmorre, for it was such a ——— of a mix-up—but I think they rode through us twice. One thing I do know was that more than once I kind of whispered to myself—

"This is the end of the trail, boy; but make it expensive."

The first breathing-space I had I naturally thought of my own section and had a chance to look around. The rattle and clatter of the machines and the erratic volleys were reassuring. Circling around us were the Tuareg gang yelling like fiends and firing from the saddle. Scattered between us were forms lying stiff on the shale and others running as if the great Mogul were after them. Fieldmorre was working a gun himself. Billy was, as well.

On the other side, Hardwicke was busy with Casey's machine—whose figure I couldn't find, nor O'Donnell's. Broughton I saw lying on his face not far from me. Some of the dromedaries, mostly pack-beasts, were kneeling in the square, with a dozen drivers and camp-followers huddled beside them, with Doc Seeger standing over them with two guns. I tried swiftly to count up how many of our Hausa had stuck—about half, I reckoned in a hurried glance as I ran to a machine gun I'd spotted silent.

The gun had belonged to Poliszkwi, whose gang had turned on him, tried to drag the gun with them and evidently abandoned it some ten yards from the camp. There were five dead Hausa, and Poliszkwi among them, surrounding the overturned machine. As I righted her and got her into action the circling Tuareg suddenly began to ride off, and as they got out of range, the "cease fire" was sounded by the Hausa trumpeter, one of the faithful.

Within a few minutes, when they seemed a safe distance away, I left my post and went to meet Billy and Fieldmorre. The former I noticed had a loose arm dangling, and the latter walked with a limp.

"Some scrap," commented Billy, with a twisted grin.

"It sure was," said I, and, glancing around, "but where's Vèron?" I asked.

"*Me voici, mon vieux*," responded a voice, as from behind me appeared Vèron.

His embroidered tunic or Moorish vest of scarlet, which he sported, was literally drenched and caked with blood, and a torn piece of his *jelab* was around his head, also dark brown. "*Sacré nom!*" he added, grinning at Fieldmorre as he drew a crumpled cigaret from his *skarrah*. "*Nous avons la veine, mes gars!*" (We've got the luck, fellows.)

Behind him came Peters, staggering.

"Barnard ban gone," he stated, his eyes smoldering with berserker rage.

"Say," said I, "I guess you fellows had better stick it out, for they may start another rough-house any moment."

"Yes," agreed Fieldmorre, fumbling with his pipe. "Will you, Peters, go and get some men and assist the doctor to bring in the wounded? Will you go round and make out our casualty list, Tromp? Thanks. William, if you—"

I went off *pronto* cursing the man because I reckoned he'd probably apologize to the devil for yanking him out of ——. Poliszkwi was stone dead; also Casey, his Irish face scarcely recognizable. Barnard and Broughton had been shot in the back. Poiteau was seriously wounded; Peters had a lance through his stomach; Hardwicke, Famitty and Sabah, besides Billy, Fieldmorre and Vèron were slightly wounded. I hadn't got a scratch. Of the loyal Hausa eleven were dead and nine wounded.

The only wonder was that they hadn't wiped us out. There was quite a bunch of those renegade Hausa who hadn't got away, but that wasn't much consolation. That is, out of seventeen whites, five were put out of mess and two seriously wounded; of the Hausa, at a rough estimate I reckoned there weren't more than seventy left fit for duty. I reported to Fieldmorre and Billy. A fine bunch to tackle a powerful tribe with. The only thing left to do was to stand fast to see what the Tuareg were up to, and bury the dead.

By the time the latter dismal job was half-way through we had discovered something else; the dying old man whom we had rescued had disappeared. If he'd been playing 'possum he'd got away during the general scrimmage; if not, Allah must have guided his darned beast among those which bolted. But that wasn't the worst—every water-skin in the camp had been slit.

IX

HOW HAD THE MARABOUT FIXED IT? Seeger was sure that the man now had been in a pretty bad state; seemed impossible with everybody around that he could have gone about hacking the water-skins.

Naturally we suspected the drivers themselves. A few were missing. But if so, why hadn't they done it before? However, it was useless to waste time guessing.

Naturally at the first discovery the doc, who had spotted it, had shouted for assistance, and we had done our best to save what remained—about half a skinful for a hundred odd men, and according to the marabout ten days from water; that was, if we went on.

We held a general council. Sabah was the only energetic voice who struck. Certain death for all if we continued on, he insisted; and moreover, taking Fieldmorre aside, he pleaded with him to go back.

"Don't understand it," Fieldmorre commented afterward. "Used to be as plucky as the ——; seems to have lost his nerve absolutely."

Several didn't say anything at all, but the rest of us were for the attempt.

"I'm for seeing it through—to the limit," as Billy put it. "What's the use of sacrificing those fellows if we were going to give in now? We ought to have figured that out before."

In the late afternoon the Tuareg came on again; but this time there was no treachery in the camp, and we were in square, ready for them. They made one rapid charge as if to try us out, and then retired and started racing around just within rifle-shot, as if to kid us into throwing away ammunition, until almost sundown. Evidently they were camping not far away. Billy put up a wild scheme to make a night sally, but we vetoed this, in spite of the temptation of possible punishment we might inflict, because of their number and the fact that they might be smart enough to ride around, wipe out the camp and have us isolated in the desert.

Vèron it was who suggested a night march. Probably, he reckoned, the Tuareg wouldn't be watching us, and anyway we couldn't stop in camp with but half a skin of water. We were forced to abandon many loads, for which the Tuareg bandits must have mightily praised Allah, in order to make place for the wounded on the animals. Peters and Poiteau were bad cases—delirious; and several of the Hausa as well; but there was no help for it. We started at about eleven, immediately after the moon sank, as quietly as possible, purposely leaving the camp-fires smoldering, with all smoking prohibited.

Fieldmorre, as navigating officer, led the way—although the lance-thrust through the thigh was obviously painful, he wouldn't ride—steering by the stars and checking the course by his phosphorescent compass. The only good point was that night traveling was cooler, which didn't make a fellow's thirst so bad; yet the cries and screams of the wounded, boxed in their wicker panniers on the swaying dromedaries, was mighty painful, for nothing could be done for them except dope, of which Seeger made a merciful use.

We kept on steadily and silently, halting for a quarter of an hour every two hours. Reckoning at three miles an hour, we ought to be about fifteen miles away from the site of the fight by dawn, and hence pretty well out of sight. Naturally they could easily have caught us up on our trail, but during the rests I could not distinguish with my ear to the ground any sign or sound of animals moving.

At long length the east flushed as suddenly as a girl blushes. Fieldmorre called a halt. As the sun leaped, in that greedy sort of way it does down there, I joined Fieldmorre, Vèron and Billy, searching the horizon ahead with binoculars. Nothing but a circle of shale and sand.

As we talked in low tones and had just decided to serve out a small ration of water, which we reckoned would leave half a cupful per man and a whole one each for the wounded, Doc Seeger came up and reported that Poiteau and five Hausa were dead.

"Perhaps better so for them by the look of that!" I commented, gesturing ahead.

We buried them there, deep, so that at any rate they should sleep soundly. We went on again till midday, then halted for the camp to rest during the worst of the terrific heat.

One mouthful of water was served out to each fit man and half a cup to the wounded. In the blistering silence of Thorpe's desert, the raving of the wounded crying for water sounded dreadful.

"I'm pretty darned certain there were wells around that last camp," said Fieldmorre once, "otherwise those blasted Tuareg wouldn't have camped there—that is, not such a crowd of them."

However, there was no sense in "ifs" and "whys" just then. The only thing that had got me was the knowledge that if that marabout had told the truth an ugly end was sure. Of course, we all knew that, and had known it when we voted to go on; but naturally we didn't use it as a topic of conversation. I did ask the melancholy Sabah, aside, what he thought. He kind of half-closed his eyes as if about to pray and replied in Arabic: "Allah is All Merciful! All Knowing! Compassionate!"

"He sure is!" I snapped peevishly.

The old Syrian looked at me—in a pitying kind of way, I thought, and I resented it.

"The infidel," he continued in Arabic, "knoweth not what he doeth; for hath not the Prophet said, 'There is no good in him?' "

"Lordy!" I exclaimed. "I thought you'd quit that stuff years ago."

"Who knows the heart of a man, Mr. Tromp?" he retorted in English.

I went off thinking, "There's something wrong with that guy; touch of the sun, or maybe bad case of cold feet"; but somehow he had made me feel uncomfortable and depressed. As a kind of restorative I went to talk to Billy, trudging along with his left arm in a sling.

Sundown came, but brought no signs of our Tuareg friends. We got under way about eight o'clock, wondering what the morrow would bring, a candid answer to the question running in each man's mind. That night was like the previous one, except that Peters' screams made a fellow bite his lips and almost cuss the poor devil for doing it. Some time in the early morning the cries stopped, and I thought that Seeger must have given him an extra shot of morphine to ease him; but it was another kind of dope that had got him.

The dawn brought an answer written in brass and steel. Not one of us had a word to say. We buried the dead. We served out the last water to the fit. We marched till midday. Fieldmorre and Billy were going through it, the former limping with screwed-up lips. I wanted to urge him to abandon a load or at least to let me help him, but I knew that the reason he and Billy were suffering—and every one of the wounded were sticking it out in the same fashion—was to hearten the blacks; with the result that the Hausa, ever with an eye on the white, stuck it out splendidly, each helping his own wounded shoulder to shoulder.

No one talked, for there was nothing to say. Except for the slither of feet on shale and the occasional grumble of a dromedary, who—lucky beast—didn't need a drink, the whole march was in frizzling silence, each and every eye fixed on the dancing horizon, slow and silent as a funeral.

When we halted, the brass and steel of sun and shale was unbroken, and there was not a five-finger width of shade. The few orders given were in low tones. Not a man murmured, save for some of the delirious and dying in their baskets, for whom Seeger had kept a few mouthfuls of water.

I didn't sleep, I don't think a soul in camp did. I pulled the hood of my *jelab* as far over my head as possible and sucked the stone of a ring I wore. I honestly think that every one of us would have blessed the Tuareg had they turned up, for the relief of making an end of it.

Maybe I've gone through worse —— than that; I know I've gone longer without water, thanks to the Mahdi; yet I don't know. At least I was alone, and although in one way a fellow feels better with some comrades, yet—when you can't do a darned thing for wounded pals I guess you feel worse.

I remember watching a shadow—got kind of fascinated by it—creeping around Billy's head. Sometimes I could swear that the darned thing wasn't moving at all; then I forced myself to shut my eyes and look again; after a small eternity to discover, by an effort, measuring the distance by a withered blade of yellow grass, that it had possibly moved a tenth of an inch.

As the sun set we rose and fastened our binoculars on the east, hoping that the morning and noon glare had hidden hope from us. In the sunset the darned desert looked like a pewter plate set at the bottom of a toy balloon in scarlet and gold.

"Come, you fellows, rouse up the boys and let's get along!" bawled Fieldmorre, fingering a pipe which he dared not smoke. "Hey! O'Donnell! Pexton! Show a leg there!"

A stir ran through the camp at the command. Figures wrapped in their *jelabs*, looking like corpses laid out, shivered into life.

"Be gob, will ye git up, ye lazy hounds o' ——!" shouted O'Donnell in a husky roar.

The guttural "arrghs" of the camel-drivers responded. Packs were lifted on to the animals, grumbling like gurgling water. ——! Like gurgling water!

The last of the moon was 'way down—dry as a piece of tin.

So began another night, knowing that destiny, as the Arabs say, was written in the dawn of the morrow.

That night most of us were hanging on to the ropes of a dromedary saddle when the dawn came. Fieldmorre had been forcibly put in a basket. Answer: Scarlet like blood and steel and brass. The silence of the last half of the night had been broken by the screaming laughs and howls of those who had been broken.

There were the dead to bury. We halted long enough for that. I took the compass from Fieldmorre, looking at the forms lying about on the shale; and, drawing my revolver, I said to Billy—

"Come on, old son, we've got to get along."

Billy's haggard eyes, in a face like a dirty piece of paper, brightened, and his mouth twisted into a grimace as he lugged out with his gun in his right hand.

" 'When you come to the end of a perfect day,' " he croaked.

I tried to laugh. Hardwicke rose up near me. His lips were swollen, but he gestured. I felt kind of sick, but I bawled angrily, I didn't know why—

"All hands on deck!"

Pexton, Seeger and O'Donnell came up from somewhere. Most of the Hausa were lying down, but at our shouts and croaks most of 'em got to their legs.

"Water close to," suddenly asserted Pexton in very broken Arabic.

But they understood, and, never doubting the magic of the white, bucked up instantly. The only troublesome people were the drivers. One fool ran out into the desert yelling for Allah. Billy shot another, who apparently went mad and tried to gut a dromedary. They couldn't curse much; and with a good bunch of the Hausas' bayonets close to their hindquarters we persuaded 'em to get the beasts on the march.

When we had got going I said to Pexton—

"Why did you say there was water ahead?"

"I don't know," he replied vaguely, and pawed at his throat. "Keep 'em going, I suppose."

Somehow or other I had hoped that he knew that there was water ahead. A fellow gets such fancies when he wants to badly. Trudging along between heaven and earth, or so it seemed to me, I vaguely realized that we'd never get the outfit on the move again when once they stopped.

I admit right here that I felt it was all up; just the idea—kind of made like that—that kept us moving on. Anyway a fellow can't sit down and die while he has the strength left to crawl. Blind instinct of self-preservation, I reckon.

Ever see a hen fall overboard in mid-ocean? She'll go paddling on, you bet, just as if she hoped to swim to Sandy Hook. Depends whether you've got it strong—that's it. Good that some of us have. Anyway we usually do, don't we?

We knew, Billy and I, and those that were more or less fit. So I made O'Donnell lead with the compass, and we loafed in the rear, with our guns handy. Those dromedaries saved us; but I hated 'em, for they were the only living things that didn't sway like a drunk on Broadway. I thought I didn't, but—

How many hours it was I don't know, nor even where that source of heat, as some boob called it, was. Funny the way you see all kinds of lights, rainbow sort of stunts.

I had worked out a wonderful theory that I was as strong as Dowie is on the preacher stuff, but that the marabout's poison had come back to stay. I began to laugh.

I heard Billy or some one—wasn't sure who it was—laughing too, like a jackass. I asked what was the joke, and some one said that there was a lake with a kind of flat-iron beside it just ahead.

I said: "Oh, my God! He's gone!"

I recognized Seeger's voice saying, "Chew this!" and I felt him thrusting something into my mouth. Whatever it was it tasted wet. I chewed good and hard. Then—

But, oh, ——! What's the good? Maybe some of you know what it is? Anyway I wasn't the only one. Some time or other I heard Billy say, "Wake up," and felt kind of ashamed that I was leaning on two arms.

Then I became conscious that the bunch was spread out all over the place and that Billy was seated on the ground making noises like a crow with a cold. I couldn't grasp what it was all about for some time. I got it from O'Donnell, who was shaking me violently by the arm and croaking—

"For th' love o' ——, can't ye see?"

I followed the direction of his finger and made out slowly—wondering whether I was seeing things again—the cool blue of forest.

During those hours I had forgotten the details of Thorpe's diary, forgotten how he came upon an escarpment which had led to the forest. I'm mighty sure no one knows how far the forest was when we saw it, nor how long we took to get there. But we did.

Seemingly we fell down that incline to a stream running down from the snows of the distant Atlas. The sight and smell brought me to my senses, more or less at any rate.

I had sufficient savvy to run around keeping our fellows from killing themselves by getting bellyfuls of water. It is true some did go out that way. And I remember helping Seeger, Billy, Pexton and O'Donnell to fill water-skins and give small *cometjes* to the other fellows who couldn't kill 'emselves in that stream of life and death. It was a nightmare; sort of thing you've got to do when you're blind drunk, and somehow you do it.

We posted some pickets, who promptly went to sleep—but we all slept. ——, how we slept! If all the Tuareg in the Sahara had come down on us, I'll bet we wouldn't have waked up!

X

GLORY! BUT I'D NEVER BEEN SO CRAZY ABOUT A TREE IN MY LIFE—shade, man, from that blistering sun. When I awoke I thought I had died and was in heaven confronting an angel. True, he seemed rather dirty and unshaven and was apparently a Mohammedan angel, which seemed to mix things; but in his hand was—tea! I had always thought Pexton was white all through, but now—

Roused up, we kicked the sentries awake under their respective trees—every soul in camp, including the beasts, had a private tree—and began to get the camp shipshape. Then we had more tea and a wash. There are beautiful things in this world!

We decided to stay over several days to give the wounded a chance and everybody else to get fit. So accordingly we set the men busy building a *zareba*.

Fieldmorre was bad; not seriously, but the jagged wound of the barbed lance began to suppurate, and he had a high temperature, probably caused by lack of attention and his exertions. Billy's arm wasn't a pretty sight. After my hog sleep I was fairly normal again.

We—those who were fit—rigged up a shelter and made the wounded as comfortable as might be.

There were plenty of chores to be done anyway—water-skins to be sewn up, packs reset and renewed, Maxims overhauled and rifles cleaned, beasts grazed and stores checked. We stopped five days at Haven Camp, as we called it, unmolested; might not have been a savage man or beast in all Africa so far as we were concerned. The rest pulled us all together. Fieldmorre could walk around again, and Billy got fresh if you tenderly inquired after his wound.

During those days Vèron and I tried to get to the bottom of the mutiny business; but although there were a few Mohammedans left among us they swore that they had remained faithful, and that they knew nothing whatever about the affair. The pagans gave another account; but it was biased, and moreover the Mohammedans had been evidently as much taken by surprise as we had been.

One afternoon I was dozing beneath a tree when I heard a —— of a hullabaloo and ran over to see what the row was about. I found Famitty cussing out a group of the Hausa. He said that he had been prowling round and had struck a big python; but when he went back for his gun the Hausa had started a fuss, saying that it was sacred and must not be killed or else the "whole boilin'," as Famitty put it, would be put out.

I quieted 'em and told Famitty they were yelling their heads off because they, like nearly all these tribes, have some animal, beast, reptile or bird, as a totem, just the same as our Indians have. In return for acting as savior to their ancestor, my sergeant, after beating dead cats for some time, gravely informed me that the catastrophe was due to the first marabout, who by swallowing snakes had insulted and destroyed their own brethren—the sergeant's—and their ancestors had sent the Tuareg after us to avenge them. Very interesting!

Naturally as we got our wind back we began to discuss the immediate prospects before us, inclined, being just human, to forget much of the past. But one thing we did realize, and that pretty keenly, was that the expedition had been badly hammered before even reaching the war-like, powerful tribe, according to accounts, which Thorpe had described.

We four—Fieldmorre, who had recovered his strength marvelously (guess he had a constitution like a bull as most of us who buck fate in the four corners of the earth must have anyway), Billy, Vèron and myself—held council. We were still, after the thorough overhauling—save a few of the wounded—a pretty husky bunch to tackle; ten whites, Sabah, and some scores of Hausa, from none of whom we reckoned there was danger of treachery again. Reviewing things, we felt rather bucked, and wondered—or I did—why lately we had been so depressed.

We had already sent out scouts, but they had reported that within three hours of the camp there was nothing but uninhabited, dense forest. We decided to trek on the morrow, and issued general orders to prepare.

Next morning, while the bustle of striking camp was going on and we four were drinking our coffee, O'Donnell came up looking worried.

"Be gob, cap," said he to Fieldmorre, "there's some devil-devil business going on. For what would I be finding but my picket turned into iligent corrpses!"

"What's that? Shot? When?" demanded Fieldmorre.

"Your picket speared?" suggested Billy.

"—— a shot nor a wound for all that I can see," replied O'Donnell. "Will ye come and have a look for yourselves? Maybe the doc had better come along. One's lying as if he was just taking a snooze," he continued, as we followed him, "and the other guy's away in the grass as if he'd tried to crawl to camp."

They were lying as he had described 'em, the fellow in the grass all doubled up as if in pain. Doc Seeger began to overhaul one and Fieldmorre the other.

"Can't see a sign of a wound," Seeger was saying, when Fieldmorre ejaculated—

"Pigmies, by ——! Look at this!"

He held up between forefinger and thumb a tiny dart of wood.

"*Ce n'est pas le nain du Congo!*" (It is not the Congo dwarf!) muttered Vèron.

"Good Heavens, I've never heard of pigmies as far north as this. Evidently—"

"That's a *pucuna* dart, by ——!" exclaimed Hardwicke. "I know 'em in Guiana."

"No, it isn't," contradicted Billy. "That's no Indian dart, nor pigmy either.

It's too short. That's a dart from a *sumpitan*—a Borneo blow-pipe, you fellows. But for the love of Henry how did that get here?"

"Borneo!" I echoed. "But how—"

"It is," insisted Billy. "Lord, I know 'em well enough. Besides, a pigmy arrow is far longer, and so is a *pucuna*; and pigmy ones are feathered with leaves—ain't that so, Fieldy? Look, this is wild cotton."

"Perfectly correct," agreed Fieldmorre. "I should have noticed that at once. That's evidently how these fellows were bagged; silent and deadly enough, by gad!"

"Say," said I, "I'm going to scout around a bit." I hailed my Hausa sergeant and called up a section.

"How far can they shoot, Billy?"

"About sixty feet."

Putting the section in skirmishing order, with instructions to keep behind my line so as not to muss up the trail, I made for the nearest clump of trees which might afford likely cover. Very soon I found the spoor of a native. But that might have been made by any of our men wandering about during the day.

I followed one which led me to a biggish tree with large spreading branches. There I found what I had suspected I should—the damaged fungus and bruised bark and broken twigs, sign which I made sure was not caused by a snake by the fact that it was irregular, whereas a sinuous body would make a continuous impression.

"Some native was up that tree," I reported, "but who he was, Lord knows!"

But my trailing didn't help any, for it naturally didn't lead to any explanation of how Borneo darts came to be used in the middle of Africa. We went back to camp, discussing futilely, and got under way.

The first trouble was the forest, in which we had to have an advance guard ahead hacking a way through the parasitic creepers trailing from nearly every tree, a job entailing mighty slow progress, for a camel is a high and haughty beast. The second trouble was that noble animal himself, whose splayed feet aren't made for spongy services and with mud and water soon tend to get sore and rot.

At sundown we were still in the dense forest. We made a rough *zareba*, and, knowing that there were blow-pipe folk about, placed triple sentries inside the barricade with a kind of shield of interlaced branches between them and the overhead trees. The moon was due to rise at about eight o'clock that night, and we planned to keep a special watch on the tree-branches and try to bag some of the *pucuna* sports.

But as we were finishing supper, at about seven, there came a cry and a shot, followed by several others. We rushed out, rifles in hand, in the direction of the corner of the *zareba* from which the alarm had come. One of the pickets had received a dart in the neck just under the jaw and was already almost dead. His comrades had fired blindly in the direction from which they reckoned the attack had come.

"There's two down over here," came Famitty's voice, followed by an oath and:

"My ——! They've got me!"

At that moment I felt the slightest breath against my cheek and saw a dart quivering in the loose sleeve of Billy's *jelab*. I, too, as the sentry had done, fired blindly and angrily into the trees, and was followed by a volley from the others.

"Get in the middle of the camp," ordered Fieldmorre, "and rake the trees with the Maxims. We ought to have thought of that before."

That was done. But beyond stirring up the squeaks of scared parrots, and killing a few of the birds probably, we heard no sign. However, men were placed with the machine guns trained on the trees. The moon rose, but we could distinguish no sign; nor were we attacked during the rest of the night. Famitty, poor ——, was gone almost as quickly as the Hausa had succumbed to the poison—probably snake stuff, only more rapid, Fieldmorre said, than the mixture the pigmies employ.

We held a council of war again before starting; for, as Billy pointed out, if these unknown —— really meant business, they could, as they did in Borneo, play the —— with a caravan in the forest; particularly with animals which were compelled to follow slowly in single file. Accordingly we arranged to have men in sections marching between each dromedary, and to carry the Maxims unslung and as ready as may be to set up.

The order to march was given. Then some one discovered that the men who formed advance guard and had with them a bunch of camp-followers, whose duty it was to cut a path, had ceased work, and that there was considerable hubbub among them. I went forward to investigate, calling for Hardwicke, who was in charge of them. The Hausa sergeant of his section came to me and said that the master was lost.

"What d'you mean?" I asked him angrily, and he replied that Hardwicke had heard something moving in the bush and had gone out to see what it was. As he didn't return, the sergeant sent four men to look for him. They didn't return. Then, alarmed, he had taken the whole section, but had discovered neither Hardwicke nor the men.

I cursed him for not reporting the matter immediately, and, thinking that surely they had been shot with blow-pipe darts and were dying in the jungle, went back to the others. We took out twenty-five men with us and beat all around; but never a trace of the five could we find, which seemed to dismiss my theory that they had been bagged by the *sumpitan*.

However, we held up the caravan; and every white in camp, angry and anxious, together with all but forty Hausa whom we left with the machine guns to guard the camp, began a thorough hunt. Not a sign or spoor of any kind did we find. We got back to find that thirty-two of the Hausa with two machine guns—which they had humped themselves—had deserted.

"Good ——!" I cried. "Then those four swine must have turned on Hardwicke and captured him!"

But worse problems now faced us; for we realized that we couldn't trust those Hausa who were left with us, pagans or no; as a matter of fact we were prepared for them to turn on us and attempt a general massacre at any moment, and wondered why they hadn't done so already.

We clustered together, we whites, nine of us, and the melancholy Sabah, and held a *shauri*. There was no talk of going back, that was out of the question anyway, for we'd thoroughly burned our boats. How to see it through was the only problem now.

In the middle of the discussion came one of the Hausa bearing an arrow—not a blow-pipe dart—around which was wrapped some paper and on the outside was some Arabic writing.

Both Sabah and Vèron read and wrote Arabic fluently. The former opened the document, which bore at the top an enormous seal bearing apparently a signature in Arabic and a symbol which looked like a kind of staff with entwined snakes, recalling the *caduceus*. It was addressed, said Sabah, to the sheik of the white infidels, and began in the Mohammedan style with profuse greetings and tiresome blessings from Allah and Mohammed.

It went on to say in most polite terms that it was the supreme will of the Master of the Faithful that the noble white infidels would refrain from entering the sacred country of the snake—whatever that meant—otherwise the said Master would be compelled to invoke the full vigor of the law—or words to that effect—and was signed "Baranindanan, Sultan of Melle."

"Lordy!" Billy exclaimed. "That must be the guy Thorpe wrote about in the ivory palace!"

"Sure it is!" I assented. "But he badly wants teaching how to behave."

"Certainly is —— cheek," commented Fieldmorre; "but—"

"I dunno," replied Billy. "In the custom of the country we ought to have done the usual thing by sending presents and asking permission to enter."

"That's right," I agreed; "but who in —— are we to give presents to? And the first thing he does—these Borneo thugs are his, I'll bet—is to try to wipe us out!"

"Well," commented Fieldmorre, "he certainly seems to have us in check, but—we haven't lost the game yet in my opinion."

"The —— we haven't!" said I.

Vèron butted in with a suggestion that we send a reply stating our objects and friendliness and demanding the formal permission. But by whom were we to send such, even if we did agree to compromise? Vèron again suggested that we shout a request in Arabic to the forest, swearing safe conduct to whomsoever should come forth to receive our reply to Baranindanan the Sultan of Melle. Billy and I grumbled. But Fieldmorre and Vèron and Sabah were for the attempt.

"Guess there's nothing doing," said I, when Vèron and Sabah had shouted their heads off in vain on every side of the camp.

By this time it was toward noon. The remainder of our Hausa seemed to be perfectly loyal. We brought up those who had remained in camp and questioned them. They swore that they didn't know anything about it. One added, under pressure, that most of those who had deserted were Mohammedans who had pretended to be pagans. Asked why, they said they didn't know.

"Guess they don't," opined Billy, "and if they do they'll never tell, for, you bet, they're under a tabu of some sort."

We seemed fairly balled up every way we turned. There seemed but one thing to do, and that was to go on with it. I took the advance cutting-guard myself, and the caravan piled along behind me in as close order as they could. Not a thing happened.

Toward four o'clock, I guess it must have been, I saw brilliant sunshine through the trees and went ahead to scout. Right outside, on the forest edge, was a walled village—a mighty solid structure too.

"That's where those sons of guns came from last night," I said to myself, "and probably where Hardwicke is."

I went back and reported. We halted the caravan, and went out to the edge to have another look at the village, when I noticed that there wasn't a sign of life; no movement nor smoke.

Anyway we brought out the caravan, formed up into open marching order, and advanced within shot of the walls. We hailed, but there was no reply.

We held a *shauri* again. Vèron volunteered to go and parley or investigate. I didn't like his going, but he went. We saw him shouting at the gate; then he disappeared within.

We waited and waited, but he didn't return. Night came.

"By the Lord!" said I to Billy. "I believe Hardwicke was right—that son of a gun's gone over to the enemy."

"But they aren't French, you boob," retorted Billy.

"Form square and camp," ordered Fieldmorre.

XI

NOT A SOUND BROKE THE NIGHT save the usual hum of the adjacent forest. The moon rose, making the small village—*ksur* as they call 'em—with its great walls and square flat roofs, with one single mosque minaret, look as if it were made of paper. But what was mighty strange was that there was not the slightest sign of any inhabitants.

When the sun was killing the moonlight we were holding another *shauri*, in the middle of which Sabah, nearly blubbering, begged us to quit right there and go back. That was out of the question, but it got me all balled up about the man.

One moment I almost suspected him of having something to do with the treachery in camp, and the next I was sure that it was a bad case of cold feet arising from utter loss of nerve—which might happen to the bravest man. Fieldmorre, who had known the man so long, was as puzzled as I was. True, we guessed he was fifty odd or maybe sixty, which wouldn't be such a lot for a man of a northern race. Of course we wouldn't listen to him.

We discussed the situation from every angle we could think of. Now we knew at any rate that the Sultan of Melle was at the back of this mystery stunt, but we could not figure out what the game was. We worked up all sorts of fantastic schemes to account for the *sumpitan*. The most feasible was suggested by Billy—that this sultan guy was either a Malay or an Arab who had been in Borneo and had imported the idea. However, that wasn't going to help us any to know the gentleman's pedigree and private vices.

The point was, what were we going to do about it? Fieldmorre suggested giving the village the go-by. But what about Hardwicke and Vèron? queried Billy. And anyway we didn't like the idea.

Billy wanted to follow Vèron. Fieldmorre volunteered to go—and I. We nearly fell to quarreling about it, finally compromising by forming up fifty of the remaining Hausa with Maxims—although we had doubts as to whether they might not turn on us or bolt—and marched the column up to the gates of the *ksur*, through which Vèron had entered. Billy hailed, but his voice hit the arch and came back mockingly.

"Plunk a couple of pom-poms to wake 'em up," urged Billy.

"No," I vetoed; "we don't want to start something unless we've got to. I'll try 'em out. You keep the gate covered."

I walked straight up and found the gate—a ponderous affair, covered with sheet iron and huge nails—ajar. I pushed with my shoulder, poking my gun in front of me. It swung creakily into the usual passage-room which, after the Roman fashion, is designed to stop a straight rush through the gates. On the stone divan were lying a few filthy tarboosh, a broken sword and water-skin. I peeked around the corner, looking through the other arch to the right into a square, the far walls of which were lighted by the rising sun.

Advancing to the inner entrance, I saw that the square was empty except for a mangy native dog which ran yelping at me, and a bundle of rags, which by the wooden bowl set in the ground in front I knew to be one of the usual beggars. There was no other sign of life.

"Mighty queer," I thought. "Probably Vèron went on exploring and got nabbed.

And after another cautious look around I went back and reported. We brought in the men; and, leaving Pexton with a section and the pom-pom at the gate—O'Donnell and Sabah were in charge of the camp—we others, Fieldmorre, Billy, Hibbert, the doc, and myself, with the forty Hausa, marched in to explore.

We made a systematic house-to-house search, but we could not discover a single man or woman or child. Signs were plenty that folk had lived there within a few hours or a day. Even ashes of a charcoal stove were still warm.

The mosque was very tiny, a little larger than the base of the minaret, pretty ancient and as usual in a bad state of repair. We looked inside and about, expecting that if any human Mohammedan was there the presence of our infidel feet would draw him.

We tried to get some sense out of the horribly diseased beggar, but he seemed genuinely crazy, as many of 'em are, monotonously repeating his cry for alms as if the place were thronged with market folk.

From the flat roof of a house we could see our camp and the surrounding country. To the east the land seemed scrub and marsh, and the horizon was obscured by thick clumps of trees. A track but not a road, as Thorpe had described, ran out from the village toward the east. Even the binoculars failed to show up any cattle or animals.

"Darned queer!" said Billy. "They must have smuggled Vèron out into the forest last night before the moon rose—if they haven't killed him."

"I say, I don't like the look of that forest," remarked Fieldmorre, examining it through his glasses. "The sultan evidently isn't going to wait to get nasty, and he may have some card up his sleeve. They may try to rush the camp from the forest and box us up here. We'd better skedaddle, I think."

We did. And back in camp we tried anew to work out a plan and solve the mystery. Nothing doing. The more we argued the more balled up we got. Sabah professed entire ignorance and began to plead that we return until Fieldmorre told him to shut up.

What the next move on the part of the Sultan of Melle would be we couldn't guess; nor what the idea was in the cessation of attack from his blow-pipe fiends and the deserted village. Doc Seeger suggested that perhaps he was going to hold Vèron and Hardwicke as hostages to force us to give up the trip. But if so he didn't seem anxious to start negotiations. We decided to go on.

As the Hausa seemed to be trustworthy again, those that were left, we abandoned the dangerous column formation and put out flankers and an advance guard. We hadn't a sufficient number of whites left now to ride with them. I took the advance guard.

The clumps of trees turned out to be the forerunners of what looked like a belt of forest in a slight depression. I entered with my eyes skinned, expecting either an ambush or some of the *sumpitan* folk. But all was as quiet as an African forest ever is. I went to the edge and signaled to the boys to come on.

An hour before sundown we were still in the forest and forced to camp. As there were now only seven whites left, and Sabah, we divided the night into two watches of four hours each, sailor fashion. Pexton and Hibbert were in mine, and Doc Seeger and O'Donnell in Billy's; and Fieldmorre was on deck all night, as he put it. We built the usual *zareba*, the Hausa working willingly to assist the camp-followers against time; also we had the shields against possible darts and had the Maxim trained high for action.

The evening passed quietly, without any sign except from the dismal Sabah, who became well-nigh hysterical. The doc tried to make him take a dose of *brometum natricum* to steady his nerves, but he wouldn't. Fieldmorre remarked aside that he was beginning to regret that we'd brought him, as he was becoming a nuisance. We decided generally that the trip had been too much for the old man and that he was going to pieces.

I came on from two to six. At a quarter to two I relieved Billy and went the rounds; everybody was at his post. I duly reported to Fieldmorre "all correct," and he lay down again, as he hadn't yet got over his wound.

The moon was away up looking like a silver ceiling with the forest branches making fancy patterns. The fires were smoldering red; and about them, with their rifles stacked, were the Hausa rolled up in their blankets. From our quarters beneath a light shelter—for we seldom troubled to pitch the tents—soon came the fierce snore of O'Donnell.

"Lordy, I've never heard a man snore like that guy," I remarked to Pexton and Hibbert as we squatted by the central fire. "He's sure enough to wake the Sultan Barinandan, or whatever he calls himself."

"Probably adenoids," commented Pexton prosaically. "Indeed he should have them cut."

"Who d'yer think this 'ere feller is?" inquired Hibbert, referring to the sultan, and that started a general camp-fire conversation.

Every ten minutes or a quarter of an hour I'd send the two around the camp in opposite directions, but each time the sentries were wide awake.

Camels grumbled or grunted; a man coughed in his sleep; some drama of forest life would set a parrot squawking now and again or another bird to harsh squalling.

A little after five, when the time came for another round, I told off Hibbert to go and wake up the cook to get our coffee and the head man of the drivers. Pexton took the left side and I the right.

About half-way around my beat I came to a sentry standing close against the *zareba* in shadow, and, contrary to orders, away from his dart shield. I spoke, and he beckoned me.

"What's the matter?" I asked.

"Look," said he.

In a patch of moonlight filtering through the trees I saw a giant monitor lizard fully six feet long. I drew my revolver.

"No, master, no," he whispered; "that is sacred."

Knowing their superstitions, I refrained. I shoved the gun into the holster and took a step forward to have another look, for in the weird light the thing looked kind of illuminated.

At that moment I heard a piercingly shrill call. I was conscious as I turned in surprise, of a swift shuffle of feet and a glimpse of the forms of the Hausa around the fire rising in the air. Then—

XII

"GLORY! WHAT THE ——"

Through a slit, a streak of brazen blue nearly blinded me. I seemed to be swaying about like a gig in a sea. I could scarcely move my arms or legs. The effort made me conscious of a head which seemed as big as a gas-house.

Gradually I realized where I was—sewn up, nigh, in a basket on the side of a dromedary, and a fast one at that. Clawing at my plaited cage, I could see a plain of grass and scrub and a bunch of men who looked like our old friends the Tuareg, except that they had no masks.

Then I began painfully to figure out things. I recalled the camp and the giant monitor and the swift vision of the sleeping Hausa rising up just before I was put out—evidently by a mighty smart blow on my occiput, I reflected dismally, cussing myself for being such a mutt as to give the fellow the chance.

What had happened after that I could only conjecture. Judging by these memories, I guessed that the shrill cry had been a signal for the men to turn on us. If that were so, what had happened to my comrades?

As the man evidently could just as easily have killed me, they did not intend a massacre. Which meant—what?

Where were Billy, Fieldmorre and the rest? Why had the Hausa revolted at that particular moment at a given signal? Collusion evidently. With whom? Whom else but the Sultan of Melle, who had requested us to get out of the country?

But if, by some power unknown, he had seduced the non-Mohammedans from allegiance and had us in his power, why had he not just saved trouble by wiping us out? African potentates weren't usually given to humane considerations.

A dozen whys and hows tangoed about in my mind, to the accompaniment of the throbs in my head and the swaying of the beast. And to every one I couldn't find a safe answer.

By straining my back and nearly bursting my head I managed to catch a glimpse of the shadow of a dromedary behind me, which showed that the time—taking for granted that we were going east, more or less—must be fairly late in the afternoon, and that probably some one or more of my pals were confined in a similar state to myself on that aforesaid beast. Whether the latter part of the guess was right I never knew; for when at length we passed beneath the dark of a town gate and came to earth—or the dromedary did—in a courtyard, I saw that there were no others with us.

A big negro, evidently a slave, released me from my grass Pullman and helped me to my feet; for after that ride, trussed like a chicken for market, I could scarcely stand upright. Advancing toward me in the chromatic glow of sunset was an individual who gave me some shock, for I sure took him for Casey come to life. There was the stubby, pugnacious nose, the carroty beard and mustache and blue eyes—

"For the love of—" I began, and stopped as guttural notes fell from the familiar mouth and I saw that the fellow was a native, evidently a Berber from his complexion and a man of high rank from his bearing and clothes.

He greeted me courteously, although naturally not giving me the *salaam alik'* (peace be with thee) as no true Mohammedan will ever give it to an infidel. He informed me that his house and all therein was at my disposal, and invited me forthwith to enter. Knowing the Arab more or less, I accepted this bluff politely and followed the slaves who were attending him.

Beautifully worked brass bowls with water and soap were brought, and even native unguents for my cracked head. Later I was conducted into a large and finely decorated room where I found him seated—or squatted—upon a divan awaiting me with Moorish tea.

He made no reference at all to the manner of my coming nor to the method of my going. We talked oriental commonplaces; and after the ceremonial, three-thimble glasses of tea and food appeared. I did fairly well, and remarked that he noted my agility with my fingers in eating in the oriental manner; but no sign was expressed upon his Casey face. He seemed to be a ghastly joke; for several times I found myself biting my lips to stop from laughing and saying—

"Aw, come now, Casey; cut it out, boy!"

In due course—that is, after we had jabbered away for an hour or more—I tried him with a feeler regarding my comrades.

The answer was a solemn inquiry as to whether I had ever been in El Misr (Cairo). Then I got it that whatever questions I might put would not be answered, just in the same style that old man Ma-el-Einen had treated us.

That's always the way with an oriental: You might as well ask questions of a wall except that the wall won't trouble to reply, and the oriental will most politely—about something else. I just had to accept the fact. And I knew my lesson, learned in those years among my Mahdi friends.

However, the fact that I was safe and courteously treated implied—if not conclusively, then probably—that my companions were also all right, and for that reason I did not feel terribly worried. I tried, if you get what I mean, to pump up all I knew about these kind of guys and hold my naturally impulsive temperament in check to play their game.

One hint only my host condescended to give me before I was dismissed; and that was that I was to be taken to see the Commander of the Faithful—as the Sultan of Melle had the nerve to call himself—immediately.

In my room that night—not uncomfortable in the Moorish way—I'll own up I got a bit down in the mouth the more I pondered. For one thing, the lid seemed to have been pretty thoroughly put on our little filibustering expedition. As I thought back, bitterly blaming myself for this and that, I realized, more or less, that we had been doomed from the start.

We couldn't possibly have reckoned on the treachery of not only the Mohammedan Hausa but the pagans as well, and all men who had come from a thousand miles away, noted for their military prowess and for their fidelity to whites. There must have been treachery from the very beginning.

Who was the traitor? Sabah? Vèron? Naturally these two names jumped into my mind. But how? And why? All Sabah's interests lay with us; supposing Vèron was a French agent, what would it profit him to have the expedition wiped out or made prisoners by an unconquered tribe?

Tired with worrying and with my sore head, I went to sleep. The next morning at sunrise I was politely sewn up in my chicken-coop, and the journey proceeded. Four days there were of it, during which I saw only glimpses; was able to note nothing save that I was one of a convoy, and that the cattle were numerous and the cultivation was thick as we went deeper into the country. Each night I was let loose, fed and watered politely—by some kind of an official, I reckoned—and put in my basket again on the following morning. Traveling fast all the time tortured my limbs and back.

After sunset on the fifth day a halt and the hullabaloo of opening gates made me aware that we had arrived somewhere, I guessed at the city of

Melle. I couldn't see anything of it, but judged that it must be a fairly large town by the time we took to get to my quarters.

By the light of lanterns, and the jabbering I got a hint as we were passing under a gate that we were entering the gardens of the sultan and recollected Thorpe's description of the place where he had been lodged.

In the morning I was sure that I had guessed right, for from the windows I could see part of a very beautiful garden. Nobody came near me except, of course, the guard outside and a Nubian who brought my food—and mighty good it was, I'll own. In the late afternoon a big Berber fellow, magnificently dressed, approached, and, addressing me very courteously, invited me to follow him.

I hadn't much option, and as I made a guess that the superior fellow himself was at the other end I didn't try to kick.

"Now," thought I, as I walked beside my guide across the gardens, catching a glimpse of what Thorpe had meant by terrace gardens, "now I'm going to find out something!"

And I surely did. A heap more than I had ever reckoned, before I was through.

I noted that the palace seemed mighty big for one so far south as they— oh, sure, the escort wasn't far behind—took me into a large hall and then politely—they were great on that right through—into a room which I instantly recognized as the ivory room of Thorpe's diary. They didn't keep me long. Suddenly the big doors swung partially open, and two giant Nubians dolled up like the Arabian Nights beckoned me to enter.

Seated on a throne of marvelously carved ivory, inlaid with gold and stones—although I was too busy to notice that then—was a smallish, swarthy man robed in the Arabian manner from head to foot in white, and on the turban was an enormous emerald.

I walked straight toward this fellow who had about him a group of what Thorpe had described as nobles gorgeously dressed, and was about to salute him in the Arabic manner when something about the eyes gave me a shock. He, too, was gazing hard at me. Just as the idea dawned on me that here was another extraordinary resemblance to somebody whom I had known, such as had happened with the Casey sheik, a swift, lizard-like movement of the eye recalled his identity—the little woman-flogger, Gandy!

XIII

IN THAT SAME MOMENT HE HAD RECOGNIZED ME and said quietly in English: "Ah! The big man who interfered with my woman! And made my slaves to run away!" and added in guttural Arabic, "Allah is All Merciful!"

Then without a movement of the head, shutting his eyes in that lizard fashion upon the men about him, he said softly—

"If it is pleasing in the sight of Allah and our lords, let it be that we speak alone, the big stranger and me."

Like a chorus came the reply—

"As our lord—whom Allah bless—wills!"

And each of the courtiers, as they seemed to be, gracefully inclining his head, filed out. While they were shuffling on their slippers on the threshold, the Gandy man did not remove his eyes, regarding me with a slight twist of the top lip like a threatening cat.

I returned the stare, but I guess I was mighty uncomfortable at the unlucky freak that had landed me in the power of this creature, of all men; and the brands of the Mahdi rankled in my soul at the thought of the revenge he was likely to try. I wondered at his leaving himself alone with me; but probably he had a gun beneath his robes. An impulse rose to rush and get him then and there, for the others couldn't be as fiendish as he would be. But then I had Billy and the others to think of.

"Well?" I said sharply at length.

"Well what?" he inquired softly.

"What are you going to do about it?"

"I don't know. It is something to think much about. But come, we will talk a little."

He turned and I followed, losing the sense of his identity immediately he turned his back, swathed in robes, as he led the way to a small door within a Moorish arch.

"Continue, sir!"

He stood aside for me to pass and flashed a mocking smile. I found myself in a corridor, down which he herded me. While I was wondering how on earth he had ever got there and trying to puzzle out what he was going to do with me, and whether Billy, Fieldmorre and the others would be all right, we arrived at another small door, beyond which was a room, smallish but long and high, with a large window overlooking the gardens.

The ceiling was raftered and magnificently decorated after the old Moorish manner. In one corner was a huge divan, with many Turkish tables in mother of pearl and gold, covered with golden trinkets. Against the wall, near the window, was a large desk—Louis XVI, I think—littered with papers. Of course I didn't notice all this at the moment—just got a confused idea as he motioned me to the divan.

"Sit down, sir! My working den, y'know." He subsided, Arab style, into a mass of cushions, and smiled.

"Where did you get that way of sitting, Mr. Tromp, please?"

"Oh!" said I mechanically, vaguely conscious that his actions were intended to get me off my guard somehow. "The Mahdi taught me that."

"Oh, the Mahdi?"

He looked at me sharply.

"What do you know about the Mahdi, as you call him?" he asked.

"Only that I was his prisoner for over two years in the Sudan," said I. "And he left me a few scores to pay off if ever I meet the gentleman. That was just after we met," I added.

"Ah, yes!"

For one moment his eyes narrowed.

"Ah, yes! That was a mistake. It is always bad to interfere in domestic affairs. Yes? You made me very, very angry."

"So it seemed," I said dryly.

"Ah! So you laugh at me—in my own country, where I am sultan. Is not that too bad to do, sir?"

"You don't expect me to whine, do you? Now see here, why not say right out what you intend to do with me and my pals? And also what have you done with Thorpe, another friend of mine who came into this country, as well as the others, German and French, who disappeared?"

"You will become thirsty, sir, if you do talk so much," he retorted mockingly, and clapped his hands.

A big Nubian eunuch entered, to whom he spoke in the dialect. The slave went out and immediately returned with a golden tray, a Moorish teapot in gold and glasses, with the usual paraphernalia of mint and sugar.

"Now, sir, are there any more questions you will like to ask me, please?"

I looked at him. Those cold lizard eyes were as blank as a piece of quartz.

"Sure," said I. "How on earth did you ever work this sultan stunt?"

"That is very interesting. It is about myself. I will tell you about that."

"I'd rather hear about the other topic first," said I grimly.

"I will tell you first," he insisted with an expressionless face, "because I like to talk about myself, yes."

"Nutty," thought I. "But what game is he playing?"

"Well, go on then," I replied aloud, guessing that it is as well to humor him in the circumstances.

"But you speak of a friend, a man named Thorpe. You did know him?"

"Sure, I knew him. I was at school with him," I said as I took a glass of tea from the eunuch, noting that it came from the same source as the glass for his master.

"Ah! And how, please, did you know that he was here?"

"His diary. Vèron—a Frenchman—bought it from a native down-country. Why, he described that ivory room of yours. Where is he now?"

"He is a nice man, yes. But I will tell you about myself."

Again that darned slipping the question.

"We will, if you please, sir, begin when we met. You did not stop to ask me why I was so compelled to punish that black lady—"

"Wasn't necessary."

"You are very gallant, sir, but sometimes much mistaken. I will, however, continue. In consequence of your hasty action I lost goods very valuable. I was not, sir, as you imagined, a collector then, but one taking from him to the market.

"However, Allah recompensed me for the evil that you had done to me. I was so fortunate as to assist a native chief to gain many captives and guns, and for that he gave me some of those guns, very good ones, and I meet very nice man from Somali—Ahab Reclos. We then became collectors."

"Slave-trading, you mean?" I interrupted, thinking, "A bright pair, I'll bet."

"It is a matter of term, is it not, sir? For some time we have very good luck, for our soldiers were very good and strong. I was still angry with you, sir, and asked Allah that we might meet again; and you see that Allah is good, is it not?"

"That's a matter of term, too," I retorted grimly.

"Ah, you think it is a joke? I, too. Ah, yes!"

And a ghost of a satirical smile came on the full mouth.

"But you were gone; I did not know where."

"Care of the Mahdi was my address."

"Ah, yes; so you say just now. Thet was a peety that I did not know, for the people of the Mahdi are my co-brothers in Islam, and they would have been glad for me to help them."

"They didn't need any help, —— them!"

"It is useless to swear in affliction, and not pleasing in the sight of Allah."

"Go on!" said I impatiently.

"As ever, the white man is impatient. But, sir, my story will be too short for you, I do think."

A slight snarl smeared his lips, and the lizard eyes narrowed.

"There's something in that," I agreed. "Make it an Arabian Nights show then."

"Ah, you are good joker. I, too, love good jokes. You have your leetle joke with me, and now Allah give me leetle joke with you, only more better, yes.

"Come," he said suddenly, gliding off the divan like a cat. "I wish to show you something—one of my leetle jokes."

I followed, wondering what he could mean. He led me through the window and down five terraces to the edge of the lake, which I saw was artificially made by means of a dam. Farther along to the right were the bare white walls of a large building detached from the palace, which, looking upward, seemed to be a long, low, white-and-blue mass hanging over the terraces and the lake, as if suspended in the clear air. Around the lake I didn't see a single moving thing except upon one of the islands a flutter of robes.

We came through a regulation Moorish arch under the house and upon an enormous stone tank cut in the rock, around which were built a series of stone seats, bull-ring fashion, mounting up to a kind of portico of Moorish arches of the buildings behind, each one heavily decorated with mosaic work in small tiles. At the upper end, facing the lake, was a huge dais capable of accommodating half a hundred men, and in the middle, was a throne seat in ivory.

I rubbered around, wondering what the idea was, for the darned thing reminded me most of a swimming-bath. Without a word Gandy led me to the steps of the great dais and up.

"This is the sacred House of the Snake," he explained with that infernal, quiet smile. "If you don't mind sitting down here, I'll show you—er—some performing snakes."

Determined to keep my mouth shut and my ears and eyes open, I squatted down obediently. From his robes Gandy produced a queer-looking reed pipe, upon which he began to blow, making weird, plaintive sounds. For twenty minutes or more, during which I began to think that he was surely crazy, he continued the uncanny melody—if you can call it such.

The stone tank was partly in shadow from the sinking sun. Then suddenly on the sunlit water beyond in the lake I saw a ripple, followed by a few others. Then far out I caught the glint of other ripples. Switching my eyes back, I saw the heads and curves of the gliding bodies of some dozen pythons.

I glanced at Gandy, seated in the throne chair. His eyes were partially closed and he seemed almost oblivious of me. For a moment a desire arose in me. Then I shuddered, for coiling out of the hood of his *jelab* from his neck was a black cobra. As I stared, kind of fascinated with disgust, I saw the snake was swaying its filthy head.

I felt mighty uncomfortable, and devoutly prayed for a gun. Thought I, this crazy maniac may tell the thing something and make it strike me as I sit here. I was on the point of getting up; but I remembered that a moving object always attracts any wild beast; maybe I'd irritate the snake by interfering with the awful dance or whatever it was.

But I couldn't keep my eyes away from it. I felt my shoulders contract and my lips tighten as the horrible thing squirmed right around the pipe in Gandy's mouth, and, getting a purchase on his hands, coiled around his head until twenty inches of the head and neck were poised above Gandy's head, swaying as if dancing to the music.

How long I sat there staring like a hypnotized bird at the disgusting sight, I don't know. The sound of a splash made me look down mighty quick. The pool below was alive with pythons, a heaving, wriggling mass of glistening color like a soggy rainbow.

Honestly I felt sick. Hundreds seemed squirming and wriggling and shoving their snouts a foot or two out of the water, swaying as if in an ecstasy of delight. More, too, were gliding in from the lake—enormous—they appeared some twenty feet long or more—a nightmare of sea serpents.

I admit I scarcely breathed; plumb scared was the truth of the matter. I don't mind any animal, human or otherwise, with hair on, but snakes—ugh!

The cessation of the weird wailing of the flute thing made me look up with a jerk, remembering the cobra. Gandy, with the thing coiled round his wrist, smiled down at me.

"That is a good joke, yes?" he said softly, and there was a stranger and queerer tone in his voice, and as I looked into his eyes they appeared dilated—kind of exalted.

"Plenty, thanks," said I curtly.

But I kept my eyes on that cobra. As soon as the music ceased the thing paused uncertainly, peeked about, and then slithered down the cloth of the hood and shrank into Gandy's clothes. Then I looked down at the swimming-bath. There was not a flutter or a ripple on the water.

"You are ready, please?"

"Sure," said I. "Where now?"

"It is late for the gardens. They are very, very beautiful. I made them."

"Oh!" I said.

As I followed him I noticed that the shadows had nearly reached the opposite side of the great aquatic amphitheater, forcing me to realize that I'd been fooling around with this snake stunt for some hour and a half, and it had seemed like twenty minutes to me.

Climbing up the terrace in the sunset, I had to admit that the gardens, with the snow-clad Atlas in the far distance just keeping the fire of the dying sun, were mighty fine. Gandy caught me pausing to look. His smile of pleasure bucked me up; for surely, I thought, if he is really tickled because I admire his gardens he must have some kind of conscience to him.

"Well, sir," said he as we reached the top terrace—I remarked from the way he climbed that he must be in fine condition—"what did you think of my snakes?"

"I don't like snakes," I said abruptly.

"Ah, that is a great peety! Prejudice, that's all."

XIV

HE CONDUCTED ME BACK WITHOUT A WORD, I wondering what game he was trying to play, the meaning of this extraordinary show. When we were seated again he began abruptly:

"I must tell you the story about myself as I promise you, yes. When I am with Ahab one day, we think that we go to a new place, where the people are very fat and strong for the market; but this time Allah turned his face away, for they were too strong and fat—you see I know how to laugh, sir—and our men all did run away. They run away for the same reason that some of your soldier run aways."

"Why was that?" I demanded, curious to know.

"Because, sir, they were of the snake tribe and so were the fat and strong people, so then they were their brothers, you see."

"And why did the others who took us prisoners?"

"Because they were of Islam, and I am their chief, yes. Everything you do I did know. That your friends go talk with Ma-el-Einen and one friend go to America to get money to come and take the land of Ophir. Yes, sir, this is the land of Ophir. There is more gold than Sheik Suliman ever did want. You see?"

He gestured slightly to the golden things all over the room.

"There is more gold here than in all the world. But never shall any one have it, for it is mine, all mine. Everybody want gold, go mad for gold, yes. That is why nobody who come to visit me can go back, because you see he would talk and—"

Three fingers were gestured laterally, significantly.

"You'll have to go some day," I said. "Every foot of Africa will be known and explored."

"La! La!" he retorted in Arabic, waving two fingers in the gesture of dissent. "Every expedition that you white send never goes back. I have guns, I have men. It requires a big army to fight me, and that is too expensive, because Germany wants it, and England, and France; and not one dares to try. Allah is good. 'He causeth the infidel to be confounded,' " he quoted.

"How did you know that Billy went to America?" I demanded, thinking, "He reckons he's mighty cunning, but I'd better leave that alone."

"Beelly? I know, too, how many men you have, how many guns. I know for what you come. A gentleman who works for money tells me how many men you have. He talked with your white men in Funchal when they got drunk. He told me."

"Funchal!" I exclaimed. "What, that darned little baron with the dog?"

"If you please. I have plenty like that. They do not know who I am. They work and I pay. For, you see, I must not have people come to see me all of a sudden, yes?"

"But about Billy? How? How?"

"Mohammed Sabah he is—"

"What! Sabah!"

"Yes, please. When your Beelly go to America he come to see me, because I call him. And then he do what I tell him."

"But Sabah's quit Mohammedanism ages ago. How—"

"Once a son of Islam always a son of Islam!" he retorted, making me think of Fieldmorre's saying. "Also he, too, in Syria, was of the snake—totem, you call it? He did not want to because he loved very much your friend Fieldmorre, but I told him to do nothing but tell me all I want to know. That he did."

"That's why he was so mighty sulky and gloomy!" I reflected. "Wouldn't give this beast away, and yet wouldn't actively engage in slaughtering us."

"Did he slit the water-bags?" I asked aloud.

"No, not Sabah. Your camel-drivers. I sent you messengers twice. One man pretended to swallow snakes, and another man you found in the desert. Tuareg, my friends for pay, I told to wipe you out. Then I thought it would be funny to see you, so I sent to tell them to let you come; but I have another reason.

"When you came into the forest I sent my *sumpitan*— Ah, yes, sir, I have been in Borneo—to tease you and make you what you call 'ratty.' But come, if you please, I will tell you my story about myself. You will find out everything you want to know before—before you will see my little joke."

As a matter of fact, these revelations of treachery right through made me feel more helpless than before, although how such a state could be I couldn't imagine. For a few moments I was so absorbed in trying vainly to see any chance of a break-away that I didn't hear what the megalomaniac was saying.

"—Ahab was wounded but I was not—*Hamdullah!* In a hut they kept us all night, and I listened to what they were talking about, and when I listened I found out why our men ran away—because of the snake brotherhood as I told you. Then I laughed softly and waited. I found a small piece of bamboo, and with that I worked all night. The next night they began to have a big dance in the forest by a pool of water, and they took us there. It is no use to talk, but to do. They tied us upon two cross-poles; but one arm was free, only one arm. Then they began to dance and from the water came great snakes, to whom they gave milk in great calabashes, and they worshiped them. Then the snakes went back.

"They began to dance around us before making us ready for the pot, for they were cannibals; but I am a Gandhi, son of a princess of Naga, and what do these poor children know of snakes? I drew from my breast the piece of bamboo which I had made, and upon that I began to play. They did not hear, for they were drunk and danced about us waving their spears and howling, but the snakes heard and they came back from the water. They came on, and when they drew near the men fell down upon the ground to salute them, thinking that they came to eat us. But no, they came, more than six or seven, and surrounded me as I played. They stopped there, yes, and danced with their heads. All the time I played. . . .

"I keep on playing. The snakes keep on dancing, for they can not go as long as I play. Then the people get mad, and they dance and howl and they break the legs and the arms of Ahab. He makes loud screams and cries; but I play, I play. They cut Ahab to pieces, small pieces, and the witchdoctors drink the blood and put his pieces on the fire and eat him, and dance and eat him. But I play with my lips swollen and the blood running until they have eaten and danced so much that they roll over one by one. Then I stop for rest and the snakes go back to their water.

"The moon goes down and the sun comes, and I am still on the terrible cross. But I watch, and presently when they begin to wake up I play again. Oh, how I play! And slowly the snakes come back one by one, and when they see this, and the drunkenness is gone, they cry out in fear and call that I am a god and fall down and worship me.

"Then I call out and tell them to take me from the terrible cross, but that they can not do, for they fear to touch the snakes which are dancing with their heads around me; for it is forbidden for them to touch or to hurt them. Then I tell them that I will send the snakes away, and I stop playing and they all go back. Then I am so tired that—I am not big and strong like you, yes?—that I faint. . . .

"When I found myself I was lying in the fetish house, and they brought me some food. Perhaps it was a piece of Ahab. I did not know. I ate. But outside they made a lot of noise and I listened. One young man, who I saw was chief, said I was what you call reborn son of the Snake, meaning the son of a great dead chief—since they must not say the names of the dead. And he wanted me to be kept in the fetish house always, because I was so holy. But another man, old, who I knew was the medicine-man because of his necklace of teeth of men about his neck, he said no; that I was the dead chief reborn and that consequently I must be chief of the tribe.

"I thought very hard and fast. I thought I would like to be chief of the tribe better than to stop in that dirty house. They made a very big *shauri* because the young man he did not want to lose his job as chief, yes? I know how these people think and what they believe, and so I looked hard for the right way. I knew that if I could find the name of the dead chief I could make proof that I was that chief reborn. The name of the young chief was Futatanga. To be polite you mustn't mention a gentleman's name. Now I knew that when a dead chief dies any name of a knife, pot, anything which has one sound of his name must never be pronounced again. Therefore I listened for some word that had been changed.

"Presently I found it. '*M'pangata*' they call the nose, but other peoples call it '*m'dolini*.' Perhaps, I said to myself, two sounds of that are the dead chief's name—perhaps 'lini.'

"Now when a man gives his son a name he likes very much to give his own name, as you do; but these people can not do it exactly, as I tell you. Consequently they sometimes try to find a name that sounds like that but is not quite, you see. The name of the young chief was Futatanga. Perhaps, I said, the father's name was like that Futatanga. Only perhaps. I had to guess. I took the first two sounds 'Futa' and joined them to the last two sounds of the changed word for nose, '*m'dolini*'—'lini'—and put them together—Futalini. Perhaps—only perhaps—that was like the name of the dead chief. But if I said it fast perhaps they would not notice. I tried. I called out loudly and quickly—

" 'Futalini, the son of the Snake, the father of Futatanga, speaks unto you!'

"They grunted and made a terrible fuss. The old medicine-man had won, and I too. I was free and chief of the tribe! The name was not exactly Futalini but Fupaluni, but they did not notice that, you see. Wasn't I very clever? You see I am a genius, yes?"

"Sure," said I, trying to fathom in those inscrutable snake eyes what he was after.

"Yes, that is so, yes. Then I worked very hard. I played often to make the snakes dance and presently I got guns from the Sudan—yes, a Gatling too—and made my tribe very strong. I told them how to fight and made great magic for them, and they won in battle. After that, nothing could stop them, for they believed I was a god. You see I am."

I didn't reply, scarcely knowing what I was supposed to say. At first I had reckoned he had some ghastly kind of perverted humor; now I was becoming more uneasy. His crazy talkativeness had calmed my first horror of being in his power, but now I began to suspect—I didn't know what, but worse.

"I am a god," he repeated, as if he hadn't taken any offense at my neglect to agree. "My name went abroad, and they worshiped me. I united all the forms of the Snake worship. I took prisoners and fed them for the feasts and gave them to the snakes. I became mighty. There were many among my peoples who were of Islam, and with them we made the others become also of Islam, and I drew them together and made them one.

"Then one day came a wise marabout from the country of Melle, and he spoke of the gold and the ivory and the cattle and told me of their history. A thousand years ago fair people had come from the east and found the gold and called the land Ophir. But, according to the will of Allah, they became drunk with wealth and idleness, and the other peoples ate them up.

"Yet again were they brought together and were known to man as the Empire of Melle, vast and powerful, from the Nile to the sea. Yet again they had fallen and now remained as small tribes who fought with each other. But there were many people of the Snake there.

"Then I saw why Allah had brought me there. Yes, I was to make once again an empire, and the gold and the ivory and the men and the women should be mine and Snake's!"

I shifted uneasily, for the quartz-like eyes had begun to burn, although the face showed hardly any excitement.

"The worship of the Snake is more old than anything in the world, the first religion. You are clever; you have read, yes? The Snake was worshiped in Carthage, in Greece, in Egypt, in Babylonia, and I am the incarnation of the Snake. Do you know who I am?"

He paused for an answer, and the eyes seemed to drill into me. I didn't know what I was supposed to say.

"I guess I don't," I murmured.

"I am the direct son of Khammurabi, the first King of Babylon, who made the laws of Khammurabi. That empire was taken six hundred years after—two thousand years before your Christ—by the Gandhies. Gandhi, the conqueror, took the daughter of King Shalmaneser for his wife. Then, seven hundred years later, the Gandhies took India, yes! You who think I was just a little—what you call—*dago*, yes? You who interfere with my business! You who smack my face!"

The voice died so that I could scarcely hear what he said.

"You have struck Khammurabi-Gandhi, Emperor of Ophir, Reborn of the Snake!"

As I sat staring at that frozen figure in robes, who looked somehow so cold that he seemed carved in marble, I felt the awful thrill of horror of one in the presence of the utterly insane. He mistook my look.

"Do not be frightened—now," he said softly.

"I'm not," I retorted, but I sure did wish I'd been able to pack a gun beneath my robes.

"I have told you this so that you can know how great is your crime, yes. Before you die you shall be sorry that you struck me; very, very sorry."

"What d'you mean?" said I, coming to myself a bit. "Is that a threat? D'you think you're going to murder the lot of us?"

"I do, yes. But not yet. I will have my joke; I shall wish you to know how you shall die. First your friends shall experience the same my friend Ahab Resol did when his limbs were broken and he was cut into small pieces—"

"——, you swine!" I shouted, maddened beyond discretion. "I'll wring your filthy neck!"

As I leaped for him he did not move. But my hand stopped in mid air, for peeping through the aperture of his *silham* was the hideous head of the black cobra.

XV

"I SHOULDN'T," HE SAID GENTLY, smiling with those basilisk eyes. "You don't like snakes, yes?"

I don't. As I've said, I'm not scared of any animal with hair on, but a snake!— And the cobra is one of the most deadly snakes in Africa. I should have had enough time to strangle him or break his neck, but that wouldn't help me any and my pals less. I sat down again, muttering—

"I'll fix you yet, my friend."

"You are so strong," he purred mockingly. "Perhaps you want to slap again, yes?"

The peering head of the cobra shrank within the robe again. He clapped his hands twice.

"You will please to go back to your friend Beelly, and tell him who I am. You understand, yes?"

One of the gorgeous-robed men had appeared in the doorway.

"Now go, beeg man, and think about, dream about how nice your friends will look on the terrible cross and how the snake who you do not like will— will embrace them so."

He made his small hand coil like a serpent. I rose, turned on my heel and walked to the door, too mad to speak. But as I followed the waiting official or whatever he was, I pulled myself together. He led me down the garden and around to another portion of the palace, which seemed mighty large for this part of the world. I tried to tap him a little. But nothing doing! He was as tight as a clam.

In a big room, lounging on divans, with Moorish tea and coffee things in gold newly set out, I found Billy and Fieldmorre.

"Good Lord!" exclaimed Billy, jumping to his feet impulsively. "We thought you'd gone under for sure. Thank God!"

"Jolly glad to see you," said the imperturbable Fieldmorre.

But I scarcely noticed them at the moment. Billy says he thought I was crazy as I entered the room, for my hood was on one side of my shoulder, and with clenched fists I was muttering:

"Crazy! Mad! Dippy! Bug-house! Nutty! My ——, he's off his head— He *is* insane!"

"Who is insane, Tromp?" inquired Fieldmorre, bringing me to my senses.

"Who? Who? Who?" I began, trembling with rage.

"Don't hoot!" admonished Billy.

"The swine threatens to crucify you fellows and—"

"Who! What swine? Here, Phil; pull yourself together, old man. Sit down. That's it."

I sat on the divan, and as well as I could, related the whole story of my meeting with this crazy Levantine or Indian, the ghastly snake business and the story of the maniac's rise to sultan. When I came to the Khammurabi and the king of the Gandhi stuff I began to blow up again.

"I tell you he's plumb crazy," I insisted. "He says he's the king of the Gandhies descended from some guy in Babylonia two thousand years before Christ."

"Well, what if he is?" inquired the practical Billy. "I've met guys who claimed they came direct from Adam, but they had to get out just the same."

"Sure," said I, glaring at him; "but what're we going to do about it? We haven't got a darned pea-shooter, and he's going to crucify you fellows alive or something."

"Oh, of course that's out of the question," said Fieldmorre.

"Out of the question!" I exploded. "But what are we going to do? I'd have strangled the little runt, but that wouldn't help you fellows any."

"Call him!" advised Billy. "He's probably bluffing."

"Bluffing! If you'd seen those darned snakes and the palace you'd guess he wasn't bluffing any."

"That's quite possible," assented Fieldmorre. "Probably he is mad, but from what you say there may be something in his boasts."

In such a crisis your nerves seem to get tautened. I could hear the faint murmur of tropical life without, the deep rumble of a man's voice a long way off, and the faint thrumming of some kind of stringed instrument, and over all:

"*Allah Akbah-h! La ilaha-illa—Allaha—wa Moham-med er-ras-u-u-l—A-la-hi-i-i!*"

The cry of the *muezzin* made me shiver; seemed like an invisible whip-lash. I shuddered, thinking of my Mahdi friends. My ——, I knew *them!*

"What I can't get," I broke out, "is why he wanted to put that story over and—and hang fire."

"Have you ever watched a cat playing with a mouse—let him go and catch him?" said Fieldmorre. "That's why. That's the Oriental. And that's why, too, he hasn't set a guard over us, I guess. Wants us to try to beat it, knowing we haven't any place to beat it to. Lots of fun rounding us up again."

"He's mad!" said I futilely.

"What's that matter, mad or sane?" demanded Billy. "He *is*—that's the trouble. The point is too mighty simple; what are we going to do about it?"

"And the other fellows?" said I.

"I guess they'll go the same way as we do if we don't find a way out," opined Billy.

"Sure," said I vaguely. "As far as I can figure out," I continued after a moment, "blotting him out won't help much, for we'll go just the same. His followers will see to that."

"Dunno so much," said Billy. "Usually when the big noise goes there's nothing much more doing in a case like this. If Napoleon had died at thirty there wouldn't have been any all-European domination. When they got him on Saint Helena they'd got the whole works."

"That's no good," declared Fieldmorre. "Remember we're infidels. They consider him a kind of *shareef*."

"But can't we figure out a plan to stall somehow," suggested Billy, "to give us a chance to get away?"

"That's true; but how?" I asked.

"I'm for stalling," insisted Billy. "If it's got to be, it's got to be. We all know that. But there's no use in making darned martyrs of ourselves if we can turn a trick and remain ordinary mortals. I ain't just hankering after a golden harp and wings."

"I'm with you; but if you're so full of ideas, spit 'em out," I retorted.

"Well," said Billy slowly, "if I were in your shoes I'd stall, as I said. Find out how long before you're required to—to cash in. The longer you can play him the greater chance we have to make a break-away."

"And if he calls me right away?" I asked.

"That's up to you, old boy."

"Don't try to look so far ahead," said Fieldmorre solemnly. "Maybe there are other forces at work. You forget, don't you, such a thing as faith in the triumph of good?"

I stared embarrassedly. I surely never dreamed of Fieldmorre making parson talk. Yet when you dig down in man you never know what you're going to find.

Maybe I was mighty dense, but I hadn't seen it in that light. The whole thing appeared dominated by the maniac's idea of revenge.

I had never suspected in Fieldmorre any tendency to leave things—well, kind of sit down in the mesquite and hope a burro'll come loping along with a keg of water. If there was trouble coming my instinct was to go right out and meet it.

"I think I know what you mean, Fieldy," said Billy. "Not to get all het up about it, as they say. Stall, as I advise, and if necessary we'll face the music."

"Guess you're right," said I a bit despondently.

But there's some kink in my make-up which doesn't like stalling. I knew it was wise, but I just didn't like it. Too bull-headed, as Billy once put it when bawling me out. But the —— of it was that the whole thing was up to me—the least able of the three, I knew well, to handle such a touchy outfit. Fieldmorre worried me too; kind of felt that there was something in him I hadn't known.

In the middle of my brooding I suddenly recollected that I'd clean forgotten about Sabah. Billy swore.

"It's my fault," said Fieldmorre apologetically. "I should have known."

"How the —— could you?" demanded Billy. "Just as much mine, for I'd have backed him right through."

"He probably suffered quite a lot, poor ——," added Fieldmorre; "torn between his conscience and his religion."

"Mighty lucky he didn't get us murdered by the Tuareg-bunch," said I, and there we let the matter drop.

"Here, I'm jolly hungry," commented Fieldmorre. "Have you fed? No?"

He spoke in Arabic to the negro squatting in attendance just outside the door, who in turn shouted to another to bring food.

We began to compare notes. Fieldmorre had been taken asleep and Billy as well. From the sound of the shouts and yells they reckoned that some of the boys had put up a fight, but they had never seen any of them since. In fact, until their arrival at the city of Melle they had been isolated. Each had the same story to relate of very courteous treatment by various village sheiks during the journey by camel.

Why we had been permitted to join here we couldn't guess. Perhaps I had luckily mostly spoken of them as my friends, or maybe our captors had acted on Sabah's information.

"Say," said I suddenly, "you fellows got any guns on you?"

"Guess again, old son!" snapped Billy.

Throughout most of the night, aided by innumerable glasses of tea, which the negro at the door supplied, we discussed the situation from every angle we could think of, but we couldn't arrive at any workable plan. We tried to figure out what had happened to Vèron, Hardwicke and the other men. As we had been treated so well we concluded that they at any rate hadn't yet been injured. We turned in about two and pretended to sleep—at least I did.

The idea that this fiend would torture them all for revenge upon me made me physically sick. I felt icy, like a fellow with the gripes. I got up.

"I'll be back in a moment," I said, and went outside.

There was no one around apparently, and I sat on the edge of the tiled veranda with my head in my hands.

My head had never seemed so woolly. Without arms, not a single gun even, we stood no chance to break loose. This maniac of a Gandhi had us utterly in his power.

I thought of wild schemes of making the darned cobra bite him. But how? And what good would it do? His fanatical followers would do for us mighty quick.

Where were the other fellows? Vèron, Hardwicke and the rest? If we could get arms and get together we could at least put up a scrap for it; but here we were like a parcel of darned sheep waiting to be driven to the slaughter-house.

Then I shuddered again as there came the early call to prayer just before dawn:

"—la ilaha illa, 'llaha wa Mo-ham—med er ras-ul Alla-hi-i!"

I swore. The recollection of those years when I had been forced to listen to that cry made me wince still.

And now? That insane megalomaniac was quite capable of torturing my friends slowly before me as he had threatened, and of keeping me alive to torture for years in mind as well as body.

I stared angrily into the darkness. 'Way down below I caught a glimpse of the lake. For a moment something that seemed luminous startled me.

I stood up, staring over the water. At first I thought that it was one of the sacred pythons swimming on the surface, but then I recollected that the water was fresh. Oh, fireflies of course!

I sat down. Then I bounded to my feet. In a flash an idea had jumped into my head. I ran into the room calling softly:

"Billy! Fieldy!"

"Hullo, what's the matter?"

"What in ——?"

"Sssh! Have either of you got any of those English matches—vestas?"

"Lord!" muttered Billy. "He's gone loco too."

"I have, Tromp, I think," murmured Fieldmorre. "But what on earth d'you want matches for?"

"Thank the good Lord," I responded. "By glory, we've got a chance then. Get up, you fellows!"

"Nutty!" said Billy rudely.

But I insisted, and explained my plan to them.

"By the Lord," admitted Billy, "it'll give us a fighting chance anyway. I never knew you had any brains before, you great big slab of beef!"

"Here," whispered Fieldmorre as I was busy on my face and hands. "Go barefoot. Tracks'll look more like a slave's."

"You fellows must be sure to get the others for the sake of ammunition, and follow the trees down the terraces to the right of the lake," said I. "Do I look all right?"

"Sure," assured Billy. "Like a darned banshee. Come on. Get busy; the dawn's coming."

As we stole out into the gardens the cry of the *muezzin* was still wailing. According to plan, Billy and Fieldy made a detour to the left while I crept through a clump of bushes toward the sentries guarding the lake exit. As I approached, barefoot, I was "full of joy and gladness," as the Arabs say, to see the sentry, with his rifle leaning against a low bush beside him, standing facing the first glimmer of dawn, his hands raised in the first attitude of prayer. I caught him from behind.

He started to struggle, but at the sight of my phosphorescent war-paint he collapsed with a gurgling groan, surely convinced that Iblis had gotten him.

Swiftly slipping his bandoleer of cartridges off, I tapped him on the head with his rifle-butt, and ran back into the bushes. The whole thing had been so unexpectedly swift and noiseless that I regretted the agreement we had arranged for Fieldy and Billy to close with the others. However, they had watched me from the cover away along and were waiting for me.

"Bully!" whispered Billy. "Workmanlike job. Say, try it on the next guy. The guard must be farther along."

"You certainly do look like a ghost," muttered Fieldy with a trace of Irish superstition in his voice. "Quite glad I know who you are."

"Right!" said I. "But take the gun and let me have my hands clear. Ghosts don't carry rifles anyway."

We skirmished along, running from one clump of trees to another. Thirty yards away was another sentry engaged in similar pious exercises. But this fellow's faith couldn't have been so deep, for after the first grunt of surprize and dismay he fought like a fury, and before I could compress his windpipe he managed to squawk mighty loud. As I went off with his rifle and bandoleer I heard Billy whisper—

"Quick!"

A voice challenged some little way off.

"Get behind and club him while I amuse him," I whispered to Billy, handing over the second rifle.

The two scuttled as quietly as might be on their bare feet around a tall clump of grass. The sentry came strutting along with his rifle at the ready and turned at the slither of grass they had made. Then I stepped out, making passes with my phosphorescent hands in the air to attract his attention.

He saw me and stopped. For a moment I had an uneasy sensation in the pit of my stomach that he was going to fire point-blank. But he hesitated and demanded, with a quaver in his voice—

"*Ka ni*?" (Who's there?)

I could see Billy and Fieldy stalking him from behind, and began to make a rumbling noise to cover their approach, when there came from close by the call to prayer. By the time the long-drawn "*Al-ah-i-i!*" was finished he was on his road to find out the truth of the assertion; for Billy, taking no chances, hit good and hard.

So far so good. We had now each a rifle—two Martinis and a Snider—with ammunition; and fortunately had not even given the alarum to the main guard if they had one.

TO BE CONCLUDED

The Land of Ophir

A Three-Part Story
Conclusion
by Charles Beadle

The first part of the story briefly retold in story form.

ABOUT THE FIRST ADVENTURE I CAN REMEMBER was with Fraser H. Thorpe, back in early schooldays. It lasted sixteen rounds, and left me with a feeling of permanent disgrace—because I'd thought of Frazer as a sissy, a student, a bug-chaser, and not good for anything except hunting beetles. And that shows how wrong a man can be!

My name's Tromp, by the way.

What he did in the world I don't know. My luck took me with other men. And the prince of them was Billy Langster, one of the wildest who ever hit the Barbary Coast. But Billy disappeared—to become respectable, I understood; while I found myself trekking through the big thirsts in Africa with an Africander named Ollendorf.

We wandered all over the shop from Bulawayo to the Nile, where old Ollendorf kicked in—or, rather, was gored out by a buffalo. The last I recall of Ollendorf was when we ran into the *safari* of a Levantine who called himself Gandy, somewhere northwest of Lake Albert Edward. Gandy was beating up a woman with a *sjambok*; so we beat him up instead—and left him cursing us in languages we couldn't recognize and could treat with contempt.

The Mahdi got me shortly after this and kept me in a cage for a couple of years, dangling from dromedaries' backs in the eastern Sudan.

When I got free I settled down—and, to make quite sure, I got married.

Fate dealt me another hand a few years later, when I found myself a widower, alone, smoking a pipe in the lobby of a New York hotel. One night I went down into the old Tenderloin looking for some excitement with Hardwicke, a young Englishman I'd picked up in Mexico. And we found it. When the fight was over, Hardwicke—between drink and gratitude—spilled the beans about an expedition that was on foot for Africa.

Right away I horned in, and he introduced me to the leader. I took one look and recognized him.

"Billy!" So old Billy Langster gave me the dope first hand.

He'd been about everywhere! New York, East Africa—where he was very nearly scuppered by a gang who first worshipped him and then wanted to eat him—China,

Peru, Brazil, and Africa again—Morocco, to be exact, where he tried his hand at making sultans.

This sultan business naturally brought him up with fat Johnny Starleton. Every one knows Starleton—he really *does* make sultans! Through Starleton, Billy met another regular fellow, Fieldmorre, an impecunious Irish viscount, who had a hunch of his own.

Between them they'd got hold of Sabah, a Syrian who had gone in with a syndicate some years before to exploit the territory back of Juby, just south of the Spanish line on the West Coast where the Sûs ends in the sea.

The syndicate had gone on the bum when an assistant funked his job, and the local sheik was made to pay damages by a British gunboat. But there were rich pickings there; and Fieldmorre took up where the old syndicate ended.

With Sabah he went inland and visited the Shareef Ma-el-Einen, ruler of the entire district. They made friends with the *shareef* and a Frenchman, Captain Vèron, who butted in while on an exploring-trip from Senegal.

Vèron warned them it was sure death to go farther inland; told of atrocities— missing men—and so forth. The latest relic was the journal of a man who had gone in and not come out. Vèron had got the book from a coast Fantee.

Well, when Billy gave me that line, I grinned.

"All right, you —— cynic," said he; and he produced the diary.

This diary-writing adventurer gave a pretty straight account of hitting inland to Nsonnafo's village; and from there on until he struck a city of "oriental magnificence" and met the sultan. Then he began to gibber about subphratries of the Snake Society—and sacrifices—and that was all. The account ended right there. It was —— interesting, but not conclusive. I turned the book over—and a name almost slapped me in the face:

FRASER HALDE THORPE

I told Billy, without any more palaver, that I was good for $20,000 for my share in the expedition. Where Frazy had gone I'd go!

We recruited our whites from men we'd known, and arranged for them to meet us at Funchal and Las Palmas, where we picked them up some months later on our own schooner, *Penguin*, and sailed for Juby.

But in Las Palmas we had a farewell rough-house when our men got in a row that brought us the acquaintance of Baron Bertouche—known to the masses as Sid-el-Keleeb, a man who sponged on the whole world until he met Fieldmorre, who came near kicking him overboard.

Well, when we reached Juby we found all hands present, except Vèron, who sent a message that he would overtake us.

Ten days later then, two hundred and fifty strong—one hundred of these being fighting Hausas trained by ourselves at the butts with rifle and machine gun—we hit the long trail.

We found Ma-el-Einen all right, polite enough in his walled town, but kind of sore at us going any farther. Sabah, too, suddenly began to balk and get sullen for no reason we could see. And we got our first taste of the real desert when we picked up a dervish—a dirty, snake-swallowing, shrieking, blasphemous dervish—who gave our Hausas (half of 'em were Mohammedans; half were rank pagan) a real thrill.

After we'd gone about five days' march into the desert sickness began to break out. First it hit the dromedaries. Then the men caught it. When they began to cash in, the Hausas showed signs of funk. We couldn't figure it out. One day as I was talking it over with Fieldmorre a spasm took him and myself at the same moment.

"Fieldy," said I, "we've both got it."

We loaded up immediately with laudanum; and the next thing I remembered— Oh, ——, I don't remember anything.

We came to ten days later in wicker baskets slung from dromedaries.

The caravan was still intact.

Vèron had succeeded in joining us, after escaping from Tuaregs. If he hadn't joined us, —— knows what would have happened. He caught on right away that the dervish had been slowly poisoning the whole outfit, and punching holes in the water-skins.

"What—" I began.

"Shot 'm—*pronto*," says Billy.

But that didn't seem to settle things either, because he had put the fear of —— into the lot of the men. The morale was kind of shaken. Irritation and complaining began to break out. We all got the infection.

Some of us believed Vèron was double-crossing us in the interests of France; others thought Sabah's actions suspicious; and an undercurrent of resentment was soon threatening to disrupt us. Only one thing could have saved us. And it happened.

Camp was jumped at dawn by a whirlwind of Tuaregs.

We fell back into a square and gave 'em ——, beating them off after a good sharp scrap.

We knew now our Hausas could fight!

But we knew, too—and every passing hour confirmed it—that the unknown reaches before us held unguessed dangers and swarmed with terrible fighters.

And I couldn't forget the Mahdi!

The action put the Hausas in good spirits, and next day we marched on.

In the morning camp was jumped again, and treachery broke out—the Mohammedans turning against us Christians, and the pagans uncertain of us both. It was a —— of a mess. The Tuaregs rode clean over us twice while we fought for the machine guns.

"Tromp," says I to myself, "this is the end of the trail."

But blamed if we didn't come up smiling, though we were hit hard. Only seventy Hausas were left fit. Four of the whites had been killed; two more were seriously wounded; and all of us had something to show.

On top of that we found the water-skins had been slit. It was enough to take the guts out of any man, but the only one to show yellow was Sabah. It was ten days to the next water, and he wanted to turn back.

We marched away in the dark.

The days that followed we went through ——. A lot more of the men pegged out.

At last when we were just on the ragged edge we found water and a forest.

We camped for several days to get back our strength and morale. And here Famitty first found out our Hausas' fetish. Snakes!

That's straight. The snake was their totem, just as the bear and wolf are totems of some of the Indians.

Well, as soon as we struck that —— forest we hit trouble again. Poison darts. They got a lot of us, and poor Famitty cashed in. It began to look as if we couldn't push on any farther.

One day a message was shot into camp from Baranindanan, Sultan of Melle, telling us to beat it or take the consequences. Fat chance of us quitting at that point!

Well, we reached a small walled village, and Vèron went forward to investigate. That was the last we saw of Vèron!

We made sure of camp that night—every possible precaution. I made my rounds just before dawn.

As I was turning in one of the guards pointed out a monitor in the shadow. I took a step forward to have a better look at the big lizard—and I got mine!

When I woke up it was broad daylight; I was in a sack, shoved in a basket, hanging from the back of a dromedary. If you'd ever been in the hands of the Mahdi, you'd know I felt —— sick.

But they treated me decently enough, and after five days we arrived at Melle.

They let me rest and clean up a bit, then they brought me to the palace—into the ivory room where Nubian slaves stood on guard. There was a kind of a throne at one end, with a little dark man sitting there with a hood on his head. One look and I recognized the rotten woman-flogger—Gandy!

The swine actually put himself out to please me. Showed me about the palace—his gardens—a wonderful pool. This pool was full of pythons, and he called it the Sacred House of the Snake.

"I don't like snakes!" said I.

"Prejudice," says he with a leer. "That's all. You'll soon get used to 'em."

Well, —— if he didn't go on and tell me he was a direct descendant of Khammurabi, first King of Babylon, and now Emperor of Ophir—Reborn of the Snake.

"Good night," I muttered to myself. "That's going pretty strong for a dago."

Then he blew up! He didn't try to kill me right there, though he could have done it with his trained snakes; but he said he was going to half-crucify me with my friends and feed us to the pythons. And, by ——, I knew he meant it.

I was taken to comfortable quarters—free to move about because, I suppose, they figured we couldn't escape anyway—and there I found Billy and Fieldmorre. I gave them the dope.

That night we pulled off a little stunt with the sentries and got away, with two Martinis and a Snider. That is, we got away from the palace, but we were still in Gandy's town.

I still couldn't see how we were going to escape; but I swore by —— that Gandy and those pythons would never get me.

XVI

"I GUESS I FEEL MORE COMFORTABLE," commented Billy, patting his rifle. "But where to now? You know the lie of the land, Phil."

"Darned if I do. Only from the palace to that snake house."

"Well, hurry up," said Fieldmorre. "The sun's coming fast."

I took a hurried look around in the faint light of the dawn turning rose, and pointed to the left.

"Better get down these terraces to the lake level of the gardens, in the shelter of these trees, and work around to the forest over there."

We started off, making the most of the cover, and, hugging the wall of the lowest terrace, trotted along. We were about halfway toward what was evidently a wall, cutting off the town from the sultan's gardens, when we heard a distant yell. After that we broke into a lope, having to hold up our robes woman-fashion to get any speed on. There was some fifty yards of bare space from the corner of the gardens to the shelter of the trees, but fortunately it was in the darkest shadows of the eastern side.

As we halted for a moment to reconnoiter within the wood, we saw shadowy forms on the top terrace against the white of the palace building, scurrying about. Of course we couldn't have an idea where we were going. But the deeper the shelter the better.

We started on again. I had not gone far before I pulled up, ejaculating, "Oh, my ——!" for in a patch between the trees, making for us, was a gigantic python, its chromatic curves glistening in the faint light. Automatically I jerked up my rifle.

"Don't shoot, you blithering idiot!" exclaimed Fieldmorre, knocking it down. "You'll give us clean away!"

"But ——! The snake!" I expostulated.

"Get out of the light then, you poor fish!" snapped Billy irritably, and hustled me by the shoulders to the right. With my exaggerated fear of snakes I couldn't resist turning to see whether the reptile was following; but sure enough the holy brute was continuing on its way as if it had a date at sunrise.

As always in the tropics, the sun came up with a jump; but fortunately the trees grew denser at every step. Twenty yards farther on I nearly yelled as I nigh put my bare foot on one of those giant monitor lizards. The beast was about seven feet long and looked more like a crocodile. Not a dozen yards farther on I caught the gleam of another snake, a small one with white and green splashes.

"My ——!" I said to Billy. "I can't stand this place for long or I'll go plumb dippy! I'd rather face the music without."

"Aw, cut it," retorted Billy. "The darned brutes won't attack unless you put your big feet on 'em or something."

With the exception of the cobra which the Gandhi wore as a necklace, I knew this to be more or less true; but it didn't comfort me any. Every moment we had expected to meet a wall, as we had reckoned that we were enclosed in the sultan's gardens.

We stopped for several moments, listening intently. But no sound of pursuit could we hear.

We hurried on again for some hundred yards or so. Then came an exclamation from Billy, who was leading. Right in the middle of the forest, tangled with creepers and undergrowth, rose a wall some fifteen feet high.

"This is the garden wall then!" I exclaimed. "Guess we can mount by way of those creepers mighty easy."

"Here's a big gap," said Fieldmorre, slightly to my left.

As we hurried after him he added with astonishment:

"It isn't a wall! It's a ruin! Heavens, look at this!"

There were several slabs of stone standing in rows like tombstones in a churchyard, green and mostly covered with fungi. Billy started to hurry on, but Fieldmorre was scratching with the butt of his rifle.

"I say, come here, Tromp," he called to me. "Look at that."

In the patch cleaned up by him, deeply engraved in the stone but worn with time, were numerous marks.

"Steles undoubtedly," commented Fieldmorre. "Don't you think so?"

"Search me!" said I. "Looks like Egyptian hieroglyphics to me."

"No, no; they're older than that."

"Hey!" came Billy's voice, but in a subdued hail. "Where the —— are you? Here's a darned temple!"

We hurried on and found him in front of the ruined walls of what evidently had been a temple at some remote period. It seemed to have been a portico, for there were the remnants of pillars carved in stone to represent the convolutions of a snake. The side walls were down, with pieces of masonry beneath the undergrowth.

Right behind the pillared entrance, if such it had been, was a tree of enormous growth with vast branches which drooped to the ground and had taken root again. We explored behind it and found there more ruined walls. As I was forcing my way through the undergrowth I nearly let out a yell as what had seemed a bunch of brightly colored leaves suddenly uncoiled and faded away.

"Darned place is another snake house," I muttered disgustedly, and moved quickly in the opposite direction.

But I hadn't got three paces before the ground disappeared and I shot through the undergrowth until the creepers, catching my outstretched arms, held me suspended. Swearing, I began to wriggle, but finding I was slipping deeper, had to call for help. Billy came scurrying over, nearly kicked me in the face with his bare foot and promptly disappeared from sight altogether.

I heard a muffled and forcible exclamation as I shouted a warning to Fieldmorre, heading for the same fate. Advancing cautiously after he had spotted my head, he dragged me out. In answer to polite inquiry for Billy to tell his whereabouts, there came a fiery exhibition of language.

"What's the matter? Where are you?" we called softly.

"Where am I? How in —— should I know! Come and get me out, you —— slab of beef, instead of yawping there! The —— place is alive with adders and snakes and —— only knows what."

"Keep on swearing," I advised him. "It'll help to lead us to you."

He did. We located him beneath the undergrowth. By tearing with our hands we finally managed to reach his hands and drag him out, covered from head to foot in green stinking slime. Spluttering and snorting, he began to tear off his robes.

"But see here," said I, suddenly recollecting why we were there. "We can't stop for a bath, Billy, or those —— will be on top of us!"

"Can't help it," spluttered Billy, energetically wiping his face on a clean patch of the inside of his *silham*. "Anyway—why not—stop here? Good— place to hide or scrap—as—any."

"That's true," assented Fieldmorre. "We don't want to get too far away anyhow, in case we can get in touch with the other chaps."

"Glory!" I exclaimed, recollecting Gandhi's yarn. "Maybe they daren't come after us here? I mean, as they think these snakes are sacred—must not be touched or hurt— Get me?"

"That's right," agreed Billy, rubbing his beard in a handful of leaves. "Phoof! They've got darned good taste if they don't."

"But the snakes!" said I, suddenly seeing another point of view. "They'll drive me crazy!"

"Go to it, boy," said Billy callously. "And when we get back we'll put you in the yip house and they'll fix you fine."

"But seriously," opined Fieldmorre, "I'm sure we can't do better than stop here. I think that there's something in Tromp's idea of their not daring to come after us because of the holy serpents. They'll probably think that their gods have eaten us."

"Gandhi won't," I objected, thinking still of those darned snakes.

"Maybe not," returned Billy; "but it's more'n probable that he's taught 'em to keep away from tabu ground, and it'll take quite a while even for him to teach 'em not to mind. Come, you fellows, let's clear away some of this muck over there and make a cozy corner. Tonight we can go out and do a bit of scouting unless they turn up before."

We selected a corner of the ruined portico, and, pulling with our hands and using the butts of our guns, cleared a small space, enough not to harbor snakes and poisonous spiders too close to us. That didn't take long.

Then we decided we'd best scout around a little to see whether there were any signs of pursuers. Fieldmorre took the right, Billy the center and I the left, agreeing that at any sign of the enemy we should give the whistling wood-buck call. But before starting I pulled off my *silham* and jelab, for a fellow can't scout in a kind of nightgown. Fieldmorre followed suit and Billy had no need, having discarded the evil-smelling robes for just the trousers and shirt.

I made my way back to the thinning of the trees. I could hear the throb of drums and the wail of some instruments. Pressing on to the edge, I got a clear view over the lake. Across the water the long white palace, set on top of this kind of hanging terraces, with minarets and trees behind and about, surely did look fine in the glare of the sun.

I admit I had made a few detours, for my eyes got wonderfully keen on spotting the difference between just leaves and just snake; and the brutes, being pampered, must have bred like coyotes; and toward noon they mostly go in for a siesta, which makes the danger of stepping on them worse.

Then I thought of the obvious need of having water with us for the day, but hadn't a single thing I could utilize for a pail, not even shoes. Nor were there any big leaves, such as the plantain, out of which I could have made a leaky bucket. The only thing to do, I reflected, was to go without until we started out at night foraging for food.

On my return I found Billy squatting, with his back against a snake pillar, polishing with handfuls of grass and leaves at something.

"What on earth're you doing?" I exclaimed.

"Polishing the family plate, old dear. Jabbed my toe on it as I was scouting past that hole I fell into. Thought it was a piece of rock, which struck me as strange in this swamp, so I pawed around."

He handed me a thing that looked like a clumsy soup-tureen, but very heavy.

"It's Mr. Snake's milk-cup," he explained.

"Has a lot more of those curious characters we saw," added Fieldmorre. "I think that this place in ancient times must have been the temple of the snake-worship. Look at those twisted snakes on the lip sides upon a kind of pillar like a totem-pole; sort of caduceus, you know."

"But is it gold?" said I.

"Betcha," assured Billy. "Reminds me of that Phenician outfit. I always did have the luck."

"You'll need all you ever had to get out of this," I retorted. "What's the use of it here anyway?"

"Do splendidly for a drinking-bowl," said Fieldmorre.

"Drink!" I echoed. "Out of that snake thing? Ugh, I'd rather eat caterpillars, and that's going some, for I'd go plumb loco if I had twenty caterpillars put on my naked body."

"You'll probably have to if we don't get any grub tonight."

"You seem mighty fresh!" I retorted; for I know snakes and caterpillars— I think I'm more scared of caterpillars than snakes, which seems foolish, I'll allow—are my weaknesses; but I don't like being kidded about it.

"Sure," said Billy. "I've got a gun again. But seriously, there's no sense in the three of us scouting tonight. I'll go."

"You won't, by the Lord!" said I. "I'd rather be in St. Quentin than stop here all night with these beasts on the prowl. I'll go, I'm telling you, and come home with the milk and maybe some grub."

"But how about locating the other chaps?" interposed Fieldmorre.

We fell to discussing what had better be done. Billy was for waiting a day or two at least to let the excitement of our escape die down. Fieldmorre contended that the chances were that Gandhi would come trying to chase us out of the sacred wood. I suggested that maybe he wouldn't be able to persuade anybody but a holy man to come within a foot of the wood, and that, knowing we had rifles and ammunition, they'd find excuses for stopping outside.

"If that's right," said Billy, "then they'll just surround the place and try to starve us or drive us to a diet of boiled serpent."

"Ugh! Shut your head, Billy."

"I think the best thing," said Fieldmorre, "would be for the three of us to scout tonight. Maybe if one can get through and back we may get some food and an idea of the lay of the town."

"Won't get far in the town," said I. "For it'll sure be divided into quarters, with gates locked and barred, like all these Arab towns."

As far as we could figure out the position, it seemed a deadlock. Finally we decided to try it out anyway, and, drawing for watches, turned in for some sleep.

Toward sunset I, having the dog watch, began to get uneasy. When the cry of the *muezzin* was wailing in the distance I awoke the other two.

"See here," said I. "Snicker your heads off if you like, but I can't stand for rubbing my nose against serpents in the dark. I'll be back at dawn if I'm still going."

And, refusing to listen to Billy's gibes, I went off, anxious to be out of that creepy, crawly world while I could see where I was stepping. As soon as I had arrived near the thin timber again I nestled into cover and waited for dark.

But just as the sun was setting in a blaze of scarlet I was glad I'd come, for I caught the mutter of voices not far away. I squirmed through the grass and bushes, dragging my gun cautiously. I heard a guttural click and a negro soldier said—

"Nay, O Fayami, not within the sacred wood, for indeed will our lords be wroth."

"But Sidna (our lord) hath given us magic against the hunger of the Holy Ones. Come, go, ye four, and if ye see the dirty infidels kill them for the glory of Islam!"

"Nay," grumbled another. "Thou art our superior; wherefore hangest thou behind?"

"What use?" demanded a third. "For have not the Holy Ones long since eaten them up? Is it not known that no one can live within the sacred wood?"

"Do my bidding, ye with livers of water. Hath not Sidna so commanded? Wherefore obey ye him not? Is he not *khalif* of our lord Mohammed—whom Allah bless—and is his power not mighty? Why fear ye?"

"Powerful he may be, but who is as powerful as the Holy Ones of the Wood, our sacred ancestors?"

"Ah," I chuckled to myself, "Mr. Gandhi isn't as almighty as he thinks he is—mostly that way with kings, I guess."

And I reckoned I had been right—neither he nor any of his holy men had any stomach to try to chase us out of the wood, knowing we were armed; and the tabu of the older pagan cult was more powerful than any dispensation the veneer of Islam could give.

The men continued grumbling and arguing with their corporal, or whatever he was; but enter the wood they wouldn't. Probably files of them were all around the confines of the wood, so that Billy and Fieldmorre would surely bump against them too. Of Billy's scouting abilities I had no fear; but of Fieldmorre's I just didn't know anything. However, there was no sound of strife, so I reckoned that all was well so far.

I thought of trying to put over the ghost bluff, as I had a few vestas still in my *skarrah*; but on reflection it seemed to me that this time I'd surely get a bullet; for more than probably they had been put wise to the first bluff. The sun had set, and it was now dark, of which I was very much aware. My nose grew so keen that I thought I could smell snakes.

The bunch of guards were still in a heap, as I could tell from the sound of their voices. Presently I just caught one anxiously suggesting that they may as well go home, for the evil spirits of the night would never permit infidels to live.

"That's right, old son," I muttered, "and means anyway that you won't budge from where you are the night long."

I began to edge my way around to the right, and passed within ten yards, near enough to have potted some of them by the dim light of the clear stars on their woolen *haiks*. If only, I thought, I could drive one of those pythons or giant monitors on to them, I'd probably be able to collect the guns they'd left behind.

But just at this moment my left hand, feeling the way, touched something cold and slimy, jerking a muffled squawk out of me.

For a few moments I was too busy wriggling off in the other direction to pay much attention to what was happening. I stopped and listened. They'd heard me. I heard their man in charge violently ordering them to search around, maintaining that a man had cried out and not a bird or a demon as his men insisted. Then came the red flash and the report as one of his men fired blindly. The bullet shrieked over my head.

For a moment I was on the point of shooting, thinking that he'd spotted me. But maybe it was a fluke; and if so there was nothing to be got by proving eloquently that we were very much alive in the wood.

Then from all sides rose shouts and cries and the swish of running men. I determined that they were all on the outskirts of the wood, and concluded that I'd best get back, snakes or no snakes. Doubling up, I made a run for it. I reckoned that they hadn't seen me, for although a fusillade of shots sounded, none came anywhere near me.

Where the denser forest began I pulled up and listened. They were making enough noise to scare the holy serpents, shouting orders, yelling exclamations and firing at random. I waited until the uproar had died down, and noted that not a single brave had made any attempt to enter the wood. Then I heard a voice crying:

"Nay, nay, 'twas no infidel but a jinnee! Stop your firing lest we anger him!"

"As long as you keep that idea in your nut," thought I, "I'm content."

However, now they'd probably sit in a bunch on the outside of the wood between me and the town, I'd either have to sit here or go back. I didn't like either proposition; but finally, screwing up my courage, I decided to return and await Billy and Fieldmorre as best I could. Anyway I'd feel, I reckoned, less uncomfortable in the little corner we'd cleared than here in the dense undergrowth.

I crept and crawled for some time with reluctance, just hating to keep my face on a level with a snake's, and then, growing reckless, I stood up and be-gan to crash blindly through the wood. Every time a damp creeper hit me on the face or hand I'd have a hard job not to yell. Whether snakes are given to swinging their tails from trees at night I couldn't recollect, nor did I ever know whether I encountered half a hundred snakes on that trip or none at all.

I had got, I reckoned, about half-way when something brought me up with a jerk—a curious wailing, dismal and plaintive. I listened. I couldn't make out what it could be. But it seemed familiar. A curious sound, like a beast whining and yet rising and falling in a weird lament.

So interested was I that for the moment I forgot the snakes and began again to scout along. As I grew nearer I realized that the noise must come either from or near the ruins where we were encamped.

I reached the ruined wall and peeped over. The wailing seemed to rise right underneath me. I climbed cautiously around, taking cover from place to place. Then I stopped with a gasp.

In an open space within ten feet of the portico where we had camped, was a shrouded figure, and around him quite a dozen pythons, whose dancing necks I could see shimmering and glinting in the starlight. My one impulse was to bolt. But I held fast and mastered myself. Then I said to myself with a gasp.

"Of course I know that darned row. It's the Gandhi himself who's making it with that reed thing. My ——! What a chance!"

The next impulse was to shoot. I brought down my rifle and reasoned:

"That's no earthly. I'll hold him up and make him prisoner; then we can dictate terms, —— his eyes!"

Then the serpents struck my eye again. I shuddered; I couldn't help it. What if Gandhi turned them on to me?

For maybe two minutes, although it seemed to me an hour, I had to beat myself into doing what I planned, and I want to say that if ever I was a hero in my life it was right there. With my dry tongue scoring the roof of my mouth, and a feeling that I'd eaten half a ton of bad lobster, I crawled nearer—as near as I dared, to tell the truth, to those dancing snakes, while the wailing and whining continued. Then, dragging my eyes from the serpents to draw a bead against the light of his robes, and steadying my rifle comfortably on the top of a stele, I swallowed hard and called out clearly—

"Put your hands up, Gandhi, or I'll drill you!"

And I repeated it quickly in Arabic.

The music ceased. The robes fluttered and the hands rose.

"Now send those —— things away; and if you turn 'em on me I'll plug you before they get me."

"They go, sir," came a voice from the figure, which seemed less silky than I had remembered.

As he spoke, the heads of the filthy beasts sank down and they began to glide away. One brute seemed to make direct for me, and had my prisoner known the agony I went through until it had passed me—within two feet as if unconscious of my presence—he would have surely and successfully made a dive for freedom. When I was satisfied that the serpents had gone I went over to him, calling—

"Now, don't move a limb!"

"Now, Gandhi, I guess we'll talk different," I began as I stopped to run my hand over him for a gun, and stopped. I saw faintly beneath the shadow of his *silham* a wispy gray beard, and the bandaged stump of the little finger on his left hand.

"For the love of ——!" I exclaimed. "Sabah!"

"Yes, sir," he responded suavely. "I am Mohammed Sabah!"

XVII

"BUT WHAT THE ——'RE YOU DOING HERE?" I demanded.

"I come here to practise with the snakes, Mr. Tromp," Sabah replied.

"Practise with the snakes! For the Lord's sake, 're you a darned snake juggler, too?"

"I used to be many years ago, Mr. Tromp."

"You did, huh? But see here, what d'you mean by playing the traitor? That Gandhi fellow says you were betraying us to him all the time. Is that true?"

"In a manner of speaking, sir."

"In a manner of speaking! D'you know I ought to shoot you on sight?"

"That is not usual with gentlemen, sir, without investigation," replied Sabah calmly.

I stared at him for a moment, unable to realize that he was not Gandhi. Somehow I didn't feel angry with him, and vaguely recollected Fieldmorre's apology for him—that he had been tortured between his conscience and his religion. Yet he seemed curiously unafraid and self-confident; apparently he had lost entirely the melancholy that had made him look like a sick buzzard.

"Get up," I ordered him, "and walk straight ahead to that ruined pillar there. And don't try to run or I'll put a bullet in your back."

"Certainly, Mr. Tromp. I am very pleased to see you."

"The —— you are!" said I. "Get along."

He rose as sedately as ever and slowly marched ahead of me to the pillar indicated.

"Now halt. Got any guns? Hold up your hands again."

He obeyed docilely, and I ran my hand over him and in his *skarrah*.

"Now sit down there and give an account of yourself."

"Where, please, is Lord Fieldmorre?" he demanded as he complied.

"Out scouting for food. He'll be back presently. Now if you want to keep a whole skin just sit up and answer questions. Where are Vèron, Hardwicke, the doc and the others?"

"In the city, sir."

"All together and safe?"

"Yes, sir."

"Have you heard anything about another white man—Thorpe, you know, who wrote that diary?"

"No, Mr. Tromp."

"Well, why did you betray us to this Gandhi?"

"In a manner of speaking, Mr. Tromp, I could not help myself; and again that is a long story."

"Is that so? Well, I guess it's a long night, so get busy with it."

"If you don't mind, sir, I prefer to explain to Lord Fieldmorre."

"I advise you to get along with the yarn if you have one and not quibble-quabble about it."

"Quibble-quabble, sir?"

"Never mind that," I snapped. "Why don't you want to tell me?"

"Because I don't like you, sir."

I laughed in spite of myself.

"What have I done to deserve that?" I asked, amused.

"That I prefer not to say, sir."

"Well, cut that and do as I tell you."

"You may force me because I value my life extremely, sir, but who but Allah may know whether I may lie to you?"

Again I laughed at the naive statement; and, having started to laughing, I felt inclined to humor him. And anyway his last remark was more than probably correct.

"All right," said I. "I'll leave it to Lord Fieldmorre. He engaged you, so I guess he's more responsible than I am."

"Thank you, sir. I have always been polite to you because you were Lord Fieldmorre's friend."

"That's all right. Now shut up and don't try to get away, that's all."

"I won't, sir, as I wish to see Lord Fieldmorre. You may trust me."

"Like —— I will," I growled. "Lord!" I muttered to myself. "I wish I dared to smoke!"

"You may, sir," Sabah informed me quietly.

"What? Who the ——"

"I mean, sir, that no one will disturb you even if you light a fire here. This is sacred ground. No one dares come except an infidel or the Gandhi himself."

"That's what I thought," said I, fumbling for my one packet of cigarets in my *skarrah*.

But as I was about to light it I stopped. Was this a trap? A signal to some one? I didn't trust Mohammed Sabah at all after that deliberate treachery which he calmly admitted—"in a manner of speaking." He was a wily bird and just slick enough to play his way out again.

"I wish Gandhi would," said I.

"So do I, sir."

"You do! Why?"

Just then a familiar voice said close to my ear—

"Who's that with you, Tromp?"

"Hullo, Fieldy," said I, turning, but not deranging the direction of my rifle. "Sabah, if you darn well please! Caught him piping the snakes just the same as the Gandhi."

Fieldmorre's bulk limped out of a shadow of the pillar.

"Sabah? Ah, yes! Had a little scrap and my leg went back on me," said he quietly turning to me. "I'm bleeding like a stuck pig. You might see if you can readjust the bandage; will you, Tromp?"

"But, your lordship—" began Sabah.

"I'll talk to you in a minute," said Fieldmorre over his shoulder.

"Here, strip that into lint, quick," I ordered Sabah, tossing him a discarded *silham*.

Then I got busy on Fieldmorre. His Moorish pants were soaked with blood; so, taking a chance, I struck a vesta and sopped the wound as well as possible.

"Heard a —— of a racket," he commented as I was binding him up. "Was that your affair or William's?"

"Mine," said I, and explained why I was back.

"Now you, Sabah," said he when the job was finished.

Sabah began a long-winded apology for having to do what was "most repugnant."

"I don't want any of that, Sabah," said Fieldmorre curtly. "If you've got anything to say, say it. Recollect that the usual penalty for treachery is a bullet."

"But in a manner of speaking, my lord, I am not guilty."

"—— your manner of speaking," retorted Fieldmorre, and added, "in the double sense. Just say what you've got to say, and that quickly."

"Very good, Lord Fieldmorre," replied Sabah with a tone in his voice I surely had never heard before. "I will endeavor to explain at great length that you may possibly understand my peculiar and exalted position."

"—— cheek!" I heard Fieldmorre mutter. "Go on then."

Sabah raised his head toward the stars until the light just caught the end of his nose, as if seeking inspiration, or looking for spiders, which was what I was doing, and, arranging his robes on the pedestal of the ruined column as delicately as a woman at a tea-party, he began:

"I want you to know, my lord, that you have always been deceived regarding my nationality. I have been Syrian because ignorant modern people would fail to comprehend. My name is Thabit ibn Kuna and I am really Aramean, which perhaps your lordship knows is one of the oldest races in the world. I was born in Aram Zobah. At the age of five years I could read and write Aramaic, Syriac—which is a dialect—and Arabic, and was well versed in the Aramaic sacred writing, which, except in manuscript, does not any longer exist, and the Koran as well. At twelve years old, my lord, I was acquainted with what you call your European languages, four of them. Since the conquest by the Romans of my country—about thirty years, my lord, before your prophet Christ—my family declined in importance. The decline began from a petty jealousy of the Roman proconsul at Antioch on the refusal of the hand of a beautiful member of my family. And at the time at which I was born I regret to say that my father had sunk so low as to be a common cobbler.

"This regrettable position was to my beautiful mother a thorn of surprizing painfulness, and from my earliest adolescence she taught me who I was. This too became a surprizing thorn to me, so that it hurt so extremely that when I was but at the tender age of thirteen, I was driven to leave my country. As I had no other means of obtaining an outlet I prayed to Allah and to those who surround us this night, and was drawn to an old man carrying a bag of gold, and with the aid of much skill and a knife I agreed to take the money so that I might be free and undetected.

"By Assuan I met a holy man who was a charmer of snakes; but I was the son of my mother, who was a priestess of the ancient Aramaic religion—of which I may not tell you, my lord, for you are not of the brotherhood. So it was that the snakes knew me, and in the eyes of the vulgar I was a snake-charmer. But he was bad, my master, the holy man, and jealous, so that he stole the snakes which I had trained, and all the money.

"I did not see him for many years, and then he died. But I had become a guide and prospered a little. Thus it was, my lord, that I came to Europe, knowing your languages. And many things."

"You sure did," I muttered.

"I dwelt in your city of London some great time; but I was not successful, for it was cold and much rain, and your laws are not as our laws. I went back to the Levant, to Egypt; and I became donkey-boy at Alexandria, but this was a part of too much exercise. When I was sixteen—shame be upon me—I forgot my mother and my most beautiful country and who I was, and married a woman of no importance.

"Many children came, and much food and things were required; so, gathering wisdom as I went, I collected a sum of money again and gave it to help my wife and left her quickly so that I might go to Morocco. And in Tangiers I met a man, a Scotchman, and having no money, for I am honest, I went with him as interpreter to Cape Juby.

"My lord knows my history with that Scotchman and with the company he made. I worked hard for them, but Allah had not put wisdom in the heart of the young man they left with me. But indeed I worked hard and was surprizingly honest."

"I believe you," I murmured, but he didn't hear me.

"But when I left them my heart was low. Something had gone out of me. Europe, my lord, has a strange effect upon us Orientals. In some way the strength to do is taken away as the sap from a tree. Thus it was that for years I lived and toiled in terrible ways, forgetting my forefathers and the wisdom of my hand and faith. Thus perilously I descended into frightful punishment where you, my lord, found me as a teacher of Arabic in London, already an old man stricken with poverty and with no faith in Allah nor any god, slinking like a small dog through the Strand.

"I was full of gladness to work with my lord; for he lifted up my heart to be with a man of race, although but for a few hundred years."

I caught a glimpse of a twinkle in Fieldmorre's blue eyes in the star-glow.

"And I was surprizingly faithful to you, my lord, watching over your interests as if you were a man of my own ancient blood. Is that not so, my lord?"

"Yes, you were certainly very faithful and diligent," assented Fieldmorre. "That is what surprized me the more by your disgusting treachery."

"I, too, am more extremely surprized," stated Sabah solemnly; "but I am extremely confident that your lordship will find me in a manner of speaking not guilty."

"Not guilty!" I exclaimed. "Considering that seven whites were killed!"

"Wait a minute, Tromp," urged Fieldmorre. "Let's see what he has to say."

"I thank you, my lord. You have understanding and a large heart, which I shall not forget. If I may be permitted to remark, your lordship would have been captured and slain by the Baron Bertouche had I not interfered in a most surprizing way. Is that not so, my lord?"

"I suppose so, —— you. Go on."

"With great pleasure, my lord. I will now come to the time when your lordship with Mr. Langster journeyed to see Ma-el-Einen—I beg your lordship to remember that up to that experience I had sunk so low as to forget my race and my gods.

"When your lordship had read the diary of the lost white man and consulted with me, I was much rejoiced, for truly it seemed to me that in my old age I should gain gold and return to Aram Zobah, I the lost son of my beautiful mother, and if it so please Allah to raise a most surprizing monumental temple to house the last of the sacred Aramaic manuscripts of which my beautiful mother, the priestess, is the holy keeper. But Allah decreed that you should leave me and go away.

"And I talked much with the *shareef* Ma-el-Einen, who is a surprizingly holy man. And he caused me to feel my wickedness, and spoke of my mother and my race. Then he gave me a message and a sign.

"The message told me to go unarmed and unafraid to the country which you, my lord, were seeking, and I said to myself that there I could make many surprizing discoveries, for by the sign he had given me I knew that I was safe from all danger. I came, and I saw the man who calls himself sultan; and he spoke much, telling me who he was and from what race he came. He spoke surprizingly much."

"Again I believe you," I muttered.

"And he took me here," Sabah continued, "where we sit in the night among the holy ones; and when I saw the column upon which I sit, I fell upon my knees and wept exceedingly, and my faith came back to me like sunlight upon the beautiful flower-face of a woman."

"Why?" interposed Fieldmorre.

"Patience, my lord; I will tell you all, that you may know my peculiar and exalted position. Has my lord deigned to remark upon the writings upon the monuments here?"

"Yes, I have. Some form of ancient Arabic, aren't they?"

"No, my lord; they are the lost tongue, Aramaic. The place where Allah has led your profane feet is the ruins of the temple of El, which means in English, the Snake, the Father of Men, the Begetter of All, a temple made more than sixteen centuries before your prophet Christ."

"But how on earth could that be?" queried Fieldmorre. "The Aramean, as you say, couldn't have been settled in Africa at that date?"

"What do you know, you blind men of Europe?" demanded Sabah with a sudden touch of ferocity in his voice. "No, you are ignorant, my lord," he continued quietly. "For your race can only feel blindly at signs. By the peoples of your kind, Roman, Christian and Mohammedan, was all the Aramaic literature of surprizing wonder destroyed, save that one manuscript in the keeping of my mother.

"What can your clever men tell of sixteen centuries before your prophet Christ? What do they know of that the men of Islam destroyed in their pigful rage?"

"But," said Fieldmorre, interested, "why do you say 'pigful' about Mohammedans? Aren't you one? You're always calling on Allah."

"I am of the true brothers of Islam. Do you not know my lord, that Allah—the very name—was stolen by Mohammed? That Allah was the name of the god of what you call the pagans in Arabia? Ten thousand years before Mohammed was smitten by Aiësha, *we* were rulers of the world! They, destined by Allah—the true Allah—were our subject slaves, and in

Africa were many what you call colonies. This have I read in the sacred manuscript, keeper of which is my holy mother."

Sabah paused and mumbled to himself in a tongue neither of us could understand. A cricket was making an ear-splitting noise close by, but I hadn't noticed it until then; and my hand touched some hairy monster on my knee which I shook off mighty quick, yet queerly enough without any conscious sense of horror as usual.

"And when my eyes rested on these things," continued Sabah, "a great big spirit descended upon me. I looked on the Gandhi and I saw my ancient enemy—this Gandhi, whose ancestors were the conquerors of Babylon before the time of Solomon, as you call him, by treachery took the daughter of the King of Aram Zobah to concubine, of whom, though he knows it not, this Gandhi is the descendant. This I know according to the Aramaic scriptures. Here upon the sacred spot, the place of the city of the queen of Sheba."

He pointed a hand toward the shadows of the ruins.

"There, within the temple upon the holy monument above the sacred black stone, is written the history of her reign. There stood a man of surprizing shameful blood, yet a kinsman to me. And I knew that Allah had destined what I should have to do.

"I did not reveal myself to him, else he would want to have me put to death, just the same of course as I would have him. He called to me to be faithful to him, obeying without question. This man of shameful birth made big oaths by the holy ones whom he does not understand; for who should know the secrets of a Druse? He, a follower of Mohammed, and knowing nothing of the incarnation of the great God Darazi, last of the incarnations of Allah, the ancient and the true god; he, boasting that he was the descendant of world king to me of the same family as she who ruled upon this spot, Sheba, of the tribe of Sabah, of the family of Thabit ibn Kuna, whose ancestors were Abgar Ukkama, the first king of Aramea and Kil-Garthe daughter of the Pharaoh!"

He had paused with one hand raised, probably in some mystic sign; and his eyes, beneath the hood, seemed kind of luminous.

"Go on," said Fieldmorre placidly. "What then?"

"What then, my lord?"

For a moment Sabah stared blankly as if trying to pry himself out of the trance he'd got himself into.

"I covered myself with shame; for I lied to him, the man who called himself the Gandhi, and deceived him. I promised to do all that he commanded. I returned to Ma-el-Einen to await your lordship."

"Evidently," assented Fieldmorre coldly. "But why did you trouble to wait for me?"

"There was much to do. Many plans and much thinking to be done. I determined that no harm should befall you, my lord."

"That was very thoughtful of you, Sabah," said Fieldmorre sarcastically; "but will you kindly explain how you neglected to protect my white friends who have fallen? And also ourselves for that matter, left prisoners in the hands of this blighted—er—cousin of yours?"

"My lord does not understand. Before harm could have come to him I, Thabit ibn Kuna, the surprizing son of the great king Abgar Ukkama—"

"Yes, yes," snapped Fieldmorre. "But that's no excuse for treachery."

"Treachery!"

There was a new tone in his voice, a snarling one. I kicked Fieldmorre.

"That is not possible for one of the family of Thabit ibn Kuna."

"Well, Sabah?"

"I was about to inform you, my lord, that within a few days the person of shameful birth shall be no more, and I, Thabit ibn Kuna, shall be the Sultan Abgar Ukkama, King of Sheba and Ophir, and of all the gold and ivory, men and women, that I may build again this mighty temple to the great god, El!"

In the hot silence came the wailing cry of the *muezzin*—

"—*illa 'illa hwa Moh-ammed er ras-ul al-lahi-i-i*—"

"Glory!" I thought. "Here's another of 'em. "

But I had got an idea.

"I quite believe that, Sabah," said Fieldmorre presently in a soothing tone. "But what do you propose to do for us?"

"Your lordship, who has been my friend and companion, shall not want for anything," replied Sabah in what you might call an inspired voice.

" 'Scuse me butting in, Fieldmorre," said I, "but I reckon you and I ought to talk this over with Billy before—you get me?"

"I think you're right, Tromp," he agreed. "Do you hear, Sabah? I'll have to talk the matter over with my friends. Do you understand that?"

"Your lordship is in the hands of Allah!" retorted Sabah; and, rising, he remarked, still in the spooky voice, "If my lord will excuse me, I will pray."

"Lord!" I commented as he faced the east in the first attitude of prayer. "He's off. But I'll keep a gun on him all the same!"

XVIII

"HE'S AS MAD AS THE GANDHI," said I to Fieldmorre after we had withdrawn a distance to allow Sabah to pray in peace.

"Possibly," said he; "but he believes it."

"Sure he does," I agreed, "because he wants to. But I don't trust him."

"Oh, yes, I do. Otherwise he wouldn't have come here and allowed you to capture him."

"Bull!" said I. "He wants to use us and that's all there is to it."

"But I've known him longer than you have, Tromp. And—"

"Sure you have; and what did he do with you? No. He calls it the great god El, and the Gandhi, the great god something else; but all it amounts to is just gold. What's the good of talking, Fieldmorre? We came after gold. Gold turns all men's heads. Let's see to it it doesn't turn ours. The complaint's older than—than the guy says his family is.

"My idea is this. He wants to use us. Let him—as long as it suits us. That's about our only way out that I can see. Work him to get our men free. Then maybe we can talk a bit; but as it is—well, I guess we're just mud."

Fieldmorre didn't seem to like the blunt way I put it.

"Glory," I thought, "he's just kidding him along and he wants to fall for the snob stunt. ——, I've got the old admiral, but that don't keep me awake o' nights."

"Probably you're right, Tromp," began Fieldmorre, "although one hates to think—"

A wailing "*All-ah*" was shot to pieces by the sharp crack of a rifle. We listened, my gun on Sabah, who hadn't turned a hair, or, rather, altered his gymnastic performance. Came a distant yell and erratic rifle-fire, which echoed across the lake into the murmuring silence.

"That's Billy coming home," said I with confidence. "I'll bet he's with me."

"Possibly," assured Fieldmorre. "You see it's rather difficult to realize that a man who has served one so well and faithfully is not *au fond* faithful to you."

"You're an optimist," I argued politely, meaning to say an Englishman with a reluctant idea. "Anyway I'm not disguising that he may stick to you, but he isn't any great shakes for Billy and me. If you ask me, he's half-drunk now, and as soon as he gets the darned sultan's job he'll be as crazy as the other Gandhi guy. They all go that way."

"I still don't think you're right, Tromp. I know the man and you don't."

"—— you know the man!" I retorted a trifle shortly. "You knew him so darned well that he betrayed us from the beginning to the end. I say, use him just the same as he intends to use us."

I felt more than a bit sore. I saw clearly enough that at the beginning Fieldmorre had been inclined to be just as rough with a traitor as I would have been myself. But the wily Sabah had just laid on the butter as thick as he knew how—until he kind of ran away with himself. But anyway it had been enough apparently to draw Fieldmorre. Maybe the "my lord" business had got on my nerves; and perhaps, too, the deliberate way Sabah had snubbed me right along had made me mad.

Maybe I was as wrong from one point of view as he was from the other,

I thought. But that's the way I saw it. As a matter of fact one of the least swanky fellows I've met was Fieldmorre—and he wasn't bent on thrusting his title down your throat—at any rate until he'd got enough to buy the usual trimmings. But we're all human, I guess, although an Englishman surely does hate admitting the fact.

The *muezzin* was still wailing the call to prayer, and in the east a faint flush was dawning while I was thinking these things about my white partner. And in a way I loathed myself that I did so, squatting there in the middle of this sacred python outfit, on the brink of being crucified alive. I had liked Fieldmorre heaps; and yet here I was, irritated over what I considered his darned stupidity.

"I say, Tromp," his voice awoke me. "I think there's a snake or something crawling up your robe."

Lord, I went about three feet up in the air; and I saw the glimmer of the darned brute, a small one, as it fell and glided into shadow. Then I laughed, thinking that after all I'd got my weaknesses all right!

"By the way, Tromp," said Fieldmorre when I got comforted again, "I rather think that you're right. This fellow seems always to have got on the weak side of me. If William agrees with us both, you'd better leave it to me to arrange matters with the man, don't you think so?"

"Sure," said I, thinking with a mighty feeling of relief that I did love a man who knew when he was wrong. "You go right ahead and fix him. Listen—what's that?"

A prolonged windy whistle sounded—the wood-buck call.

"That's Billy," said I, and returned it.

Within a few minutes Langster showed up in the rose-pallid light, bearing what looked like a bag of loot. As it happened, he saw Sabah first, still praying his head off, dropped the bag and switched his rifle around. I called out to him that it was all right. He hesitated a moment, and at Fieldmorre's assurance as well, picked up his load and came on.

"What in —— is that —— —— doing alive?" he demanded as he approached the wall, and I couldn't help feeling a glow of satisfaction.

I left it to Fieldmorre to explain. Billy didn't seem pleased, and grumbled—

"Anyway the swine made me upset half the water I had!"

Billy related briefly that the row which I had caused had evidently drawn away the soldiers and that he had walked through into the town as easily, as he put it, as strolling down Fifth Avenue. He had found himself in a quarter of the *millah* ("Salted Quarter" of the Jews). Nobody was about, for Jews were allowed neither to ride nor be out after sunset.

He had broken into a house at random, where he had held up a patriarch and the whole family—had explained as much as he thought fit and demanded food, *et cetera*. Apparently he hadn't needed his rifle.

Although he was somewhat reticent about the affair, we gathered that as he hadn't expected us home till the dawn, expressly stated, he had consented to accept the hospitality of the patriarch and incidentally his pretty daughters. Trust Billy for that!

He had, so he said, spent the whole night in sounding the head of the family. Here, as in all, or nearly all, Mohammedan towns I have ever known or heard of, there were Jews who are always persecuted by the Mohammedans and always have more money than all the others. What they had in the way of goldware was enough to make a pirate swoon, said Billy. However, he had not succeeded as far as he knew in making any practical arrangement for getting away; solely, he insisted, because they were so almighty scared. So Billy.

Anyway we were always good—through Billy apparently—for food and water and also wine of a crude and fierce variety, as he proved. However, on the way back he had found the heroes at their posts and had had to pot the gentleman who opposed his road, the ensuing uproar being the fusillade after him into the sacred wood where, as Sabah had said, none dared to follow.

In the mean time the sun had come and Sabah had finished his devotions, to which Allah I never could determine; but as there are in Islam, as in other religions, sixty-and-seven different sects, I suppose it wasn't of much importance. Having suggested that Fieldmorre explain the position to Billy, I undertook to entertain the king of the bugs, as I irreverently called him.

I walked back to meet Sabah as he picked up his prayer carpet, and for our own nefarious purposes said as politely as I knew how:

"See here, Sabah, Lord Fieldmorre and my friend who's just come back want to talk the matter over. If you—um— Watch the sunrise with me, huh?"

Sabah looked at me. He had turned and was facing the east again; the blood glow of the sun was on his face. The eyes and the features which had been like those of an old man were twenty years younger; his flesh seemed firm, and the network of wrinkles was clean wiped out. I remember kind of staring at him and thinking—

"Glory, the poets talk about love; but that's no kind of dope like this!"

He looked at me and quietly sat on the ruined wall; and at the moment Fox, the film man, if he could have seen him, would have given half a million bucks to have him pose as John the Baptist. I'll admit I felt uncomfortable. I'm no diplomat anyway, which fact Billy is too fond of rubbing in to me. Said Sabah—

"You don't—like me, Mr. Tromp."

"I don't, Sabah!" said I, nearly laughing. "But you don't like me, as you were so mighty kind to point out."

"It is impossible!"

"I'm with you," I agreed heartily.

"You do not understand, as it is impossible that the West shall understand the East."

"How about Lord Fieldmorre then?" I queried, wondering what he'd say.

"He comes from the East, for he is of an ancient family, a Celt. But yet he is ruined. For you of the West build your houses on the future, which is sand; and we of the East build on the past, which is rock."

Somehow I reckon my slumbering democratic spirit was riled. I felt kind of mad with all this king and lord stuff.

"Now say, Sabah," said I, "if you want to talk, that's what we'd call sophistry. You seem to think that every guy in the States is some sort of a cross between a dago and a squarehead. Now I'm not given to showing the high spots; but as for family, ——, man! If you must know, my mother was Queen of the Gas-House Gang and my father was the Prince of the Ten Der Loin. His father was the Duke Bronx, who was descended from an illegitimate son of Charlemagne. You've heard of him, haven't you, Sabah?"

"Yes, sir, I have read of him."

"Well, Charlemagne was the direct descendant of Bay Bee Doll, the King of the Ya Hoos. Get that?"

"Yes, sir. And the Ya Hoos?" said Sabah in a distinctly different voice. "Were they of an eastern race?"

"Sure they were," said I solemnly. "The first Aryan race, who, as you must know, came from the Mesopotamian Valley. My great ancestor, Bay Bee Doll, was the king who reigned in the seventeenth century before Christ. Now that's got you beat, hasn't it?"

"I am very glad, sir," responded Sabah gravely, and, turning to a tablet he began wiping away the fungus and creepers.

Presently when Billy and Fieldmorre were through they called to me.

"Say, Phil," said Billy when I had joined them, keeping a weather eye on Sabah, who was still busy with the writing. "Fieldy and I reckon that we'd better try to fix things with Sabah. I suggested putting a gun up against him and making him swear to our terms, but Fieldy reckoned he'd swear his head off to save his hide and go back on us afterward if it suited him."

"That's right," I agreed. "He sure would, the rat!"

"By merely shooting him—as he deserves, I admit—we are just where we were before," butted in Fieldmorre. "My point is that only by appealing to his better side can we hope to get anything from him."

"Better side!" I scoffed. "He don't own any sich animile! But go to it. It's as good as any other scheme."

"Anyway," continued Billy, "if he gets the sultan's job we sha'n't run such a risk of being crucified. Are you with us?"

"Sure," said I; "but all the same, keep an eye on him."

"Well, I guess it's that or nothing. Apparently we can stay right here indefinitely, but that won't get us anywhere; or if we do break out—and we can't without the boys—we'd never get through them, the desert and the Tuareg as well."

"That's what I say," assented Billy; "and moreover it's no time to play for anything but getting our bunch free again. If we can do that and raise some guns, I reckon we may yet be able to talk."

Fieldmorre called Sabah and demanded what he intended to do.

"If you gentlemen will stop here until you hear from me for two days," said Sabah, "you will hear surprizing news, for I shall be sultan."

"That's all right," said Billy. "But what about our pals?"

"I will see after them, Mr. Langster."

"And Thorpe?" I queried.

"I will cause many inquiries to be made to see whether he is still alive, sir."

"But how do you propose, Sabah," inquired Fieldmorre, "to become sultan with such extraordinary rapidity; eh?"

"Tomorrow night, my lord, there is a great festival at the temple this man has made, when this Gandhi person will call the sacred serpents from this wood."

"Thank the good Lord!" I interrupted. "Guess I'll have one night of peace!"

"And then," continued Sabah, "I will prove that he is an impostor, a man of shameful birth, and that I am the true king of surprizing power and might."

"How are you going to do that?" I queried, skeptically I suppose.

"That, Mr. Tromp," he retorted with a return of the haughty manner, "can be known only to the initiated of the brethren."

"Go to it!" urged Billy, squashing me with a look. "But where do we come in? We're to stop here while the show's on. Is that the idea?"

It was, according to Sabah.

Fieldmorre again demanded to know how he proposed to protect our men from any atrocities the Gandhi might take it into his head to do. Sabah's replies seemed mighty vague and wabbly. I watched him disappear into the forest with many misgivings. As soon, thought I, as he's got a whack of gilded pomp and power in his nut, he'll go just as crazy as the other guy to prevent news of his darned empire of gold and ivory, men and women, getting through to any of the big land-grabbers; and to do that he'd just have to adopt as murderous a policy as the Gandhi man.

"What gets me," remarked Billy, discussing the situation as we fed on Billy's loot from the Jews, "is how he reckons he's going to turn the sultan trick in five minutes. 'Smatter of fact, I reckon he's as mad as t'other guy. And I surely would love to put him up against that wall over there and let him have what he's asked for. To think of our fellows lying 'way back, and the whole expedition, guns and everything, in the hands of that little Levantine rat, as you call him, just because this other little runt went back on us, makes me hot in the collar."

"Well, Langster," said Fieldmorre coldly, "I've already apologized for my error of judgment in engaging the man, but no one on earth could possibly have foreseen that—"

"Oh, quit it, Fieldy!" retorted Billy. "I've nothing on you. Good Lord, aren't we all in the same boat? Wasn't I as much to blame as you? I'd have bet my shirt that he was straight—until he began the sulky business 'way back. Then I did think it was queer. Let's drop the subject anyway. Here, have some more *Château de Juif*, old dear!"

As a matter of fact we were all pretty well fagged out and by his eyes I reckoned Fieldmorre's busted wound was giving him ——. As before, we divided the day into watches. The other two, covering their faces with their robes, rolled up in the shade, leaving me on deck as I had done the least.

I did some intensive thinking trying out the position from every angle I could imagine, and the more I pondered the less confidence I had in Sabah. I'm always willing to try everything once, but after the first time I never trust a man once he's let me down, on the principle that if he'll do it once he'll surely do it three times if he gets the chance. I had decided before my watch was up that I at any rate would go along to see the show and what they were up to.

As I awoke the first thing I noticed was the pulse of drums and the wail of some reed instruments. I sat up and pulled my *silham* off my face. It was late. The dying sun was blooding the tops of the trees. Billy was still curled up beside me.

I stood up, but I couldn't see Fieldmorre. I called, but there was no response. I awoke Billy. We shouted and hunted around, but Fieldmorre had disappeared. Then, as I was standing on the top of a stele, and Billy was saying that we'd better snout around deeper in the forest, we started as his voice bellowed seemingly close to us:

"Langster! Tromp! I'm—"

The shout ended in a gurgle.

XIX

WE BOTH MADE A DASH IN DIFFERENT DIRECTIONS, but discovered no sign of any human being.

"The shout came from here," I insisted as we met again.

"It didn't, you darned idiot," snapped Billy. "It was to my right. Somewhere over there."

We were both convinced that the call had come from contrary points. In the mean time the light was failing rapidly.

"Well, I guess it's no use disputing," said I. "What're we going to do about it? Queer he didn't get a chance to shoot."

"He's been kidnapped," declared Billy. "For if he'd been shot, wounded or killed we should have heard it, and he'd be around somewhere. Anyway that's my hunch. We'll make a thorough search of these ruins. Appears to me as if some one stalked up under cover."

"It's too late," said I as the brief twilight went out. "I've got an idea. If, as you say, he's been kidnapped they can't have got far with him. Let's cast around a bit in a circle."

"What's the good of that? You'll never find his trail if you crossed it in the dark?"

"That's true," I had to admit. "You stop here and I'll make a throw anyway," I added obstinately, although I had no stomach for crawling about in this snake park in the dark.

I went off, carrying my convoy of mosquitoes with me, made my way to the thinning of the timber and by a detour to the left, and came back without finding anything beyond the fact that the cordon of guards was still squatting around us.

To my relief Billy was awaiting me, but without news. Crouching beside our bit of ruined wall, we settled down for the night, sometimes discussing in a whisper Fieldmorre's fate, but mostly watching and listening intently in opposite directions. Somewhere about midnight Billy suddenly fired and leaped over the wall, shouting—

"Keep me covered!"

Wondering what he had seen, I did so, and heard him breaking about in the bushes. Presently he returned, swearing.

"Must have missed him," he told me, "for I sure saw the white robes of a man beyond that tree there."

Throughout the remainder of the night, except for the hum of mosquitoes and the distant drums, there was no disturbance. Dawn came at last, and while waiting for the sun we hastily ate and drank. Then we made for the spot where Billy had sworn he had seen some one. He was right, for a trail of broken branches and trampled grass was plain. Not ten yards along Billy gave a whoop.

"Got him! Look, there's his blood!"

"Or is it Fieldmorre's?" I queried.

The trail led directly into the dense thicket which we had taken for dense jungle when cursorily passing it before. Thirty yards within, we came upon another ruined wall and found ourselves in what had evidently been the courtyard of a great temple abandoned for long, as was evidenced by the presence of great trees and dense vegetation. Here we came upon a spot soaked with blood, eloquently proving that the man had been badly wounded and had been compelled to rest awhile.

Deeper in, following the blood spoor, we came upon another kind of portico of serpentine columns in a better state of preservation than the first we had found. Within this was the body of the temple, with fairly high ruins of the walls. The roof, if ever there had been one, had long since gone, but there were abundant signs that human beings used the place.

And on the far side, amid a small forest of young trees, rose a tall, round shaft jutting up from two great black stones, evidently used as a kind of altar, sprawling upon which was the form of a man dressed in peculiar-color robes such as we had never seen before, and a green turban.

"Must be a priest," commented Billy after examining the corpse, which had been shot through the lungs. "That would account for his daring to enter the sacred grove. I guess he or his fellows must have kidnapped Fieldy. There must be a way out—through the back probably. Come on."

But before going, I gave a glance at the shaft, which was polished and covered with what Sabah had declared were Aramaic characters relating the history of the Queen of Sheba; and from the general form of the monument and drawings upon part of the walls I saw that the python was symbol of the primitive nature worship. Also I remarked that before the black stones where lay the dead man the ground was cleared and beaten flat by many feet, suggesting that there was perhaps an inner cult which still used the old temple in preference to the one erected by the Gandhi.

As Billy had guessed, from a corner of the ruined temple a distinct trail led through some creepers, evidently purposely left to mask the path, to a hole in the wall. After scouting cautiously beyond, we went through and found ourselves in dense jungle on quite a well-beaten path.

"Say, Billy," said I, "they must have carried off Fieldmorre along this path. I guess we'd better go along and investigate."

"That's right," he agreed; "and what's more, I'm for taking a chance. See if we can get into the town and to my Jews. Maybe I can persuade 'em to fix us up with some disguise."

"I'm with you. Tonight the show, according to Sabah, and I am determined to see that out anyway. But, Billy, Jew clothes won't be any good. They sure won't let Jews into their movie palace."

"Course not, but they can get other gear. Send out the girl to buy it. The only point is, how're we going to get through the guards? The timber runs pretty close up to the old wall of the *millah*. It's partly ruined, and I found an easy gap to scramble through. Anyway we'll see. Come along."

On the edge of the dense jungle we could see through the light timber a group of three guards squatting in the shade of an angle of a buttress of the wall. The next group was out of sight as far as we could see after a bit of scouting.

"There's only one way," said I. "That, I reckon, is to stalk near enough for a sure shot. You take one and I another and both the third as he tries to bolt, which he surely will."

By careful crawling we drew to the edge of the light timber. Beyond there was no cover at all, and some sixty or seventy yards of soggy ground between us and the guard, who appeared, we could now see, to be playing some kind of game.

"You take the fellow in the far corner," whispered Billy. "If that other guy would kindly move his head about four inches I might get 'em both."

Even as he spoke, the man, in leaning forward to play, unwittingly complied. Billy fired a fraction of a second before I did, My man crumpled into the corner where he was sitting. Looking, I saw that both Billy's men had leaped to their feet. One swung round and pitched on to his face; but the other, apparently mad with fright, charged straight toward us. Billy dropped him half-way.

"Now run like the ——," he called, "before they get after us."

Billy had in fact mighty nigh got two in one shot, for as we passed, I saw the man who'd started charging us had a gash right across his eyes, which had surely blinded him instantly. As we gained the broken gap a little to the left we heard shouts and saw some other guards running round the wood. Whether they had seen us or not we couldn't judge.

As I dropped after Billy into the dirty street of the quarter, a young Jew and a donkey turned the corner. Billy brought his rifle up. The man squawked and fled, leaving his laden donkey. We stopped a moment to put on our slippers, for no one but a slave or a Jew would walk barefoot in a town.

"Now we get into a bazaar street," said Billy. "One thing, they'll think we're Arabs and won't scarce dare look at us. My old pal lives down a side lane beyond here."

The market street was crowded with men and women, the men all wearing black *soutanes* and embroidered yellow slippers, and the women red ones, as here in their own quarters they were allowed to do so.

The tiny shops, about three feet from the ground beneath the ragged and broken mats stretched overhead as an awning from house to house, were still crowded with the morning marketers. Except for cringing out of our way as we swaggered slowly along—for speed on foot would have been suspicious— scarcely a man looked at us. Without incident we arrived before the usual iron-studded gates of a Moorish house but painted Jewish style a bright blue.

Holding our guns beneath our robes in order not to scare the inmates, Billy thumped on the door, and to the negro slave who appeared, demanded in a grumbling, guttural Arabic to see the master. We were shown into the usual guest-room, not forgetting to leave our slippers on the threshold, and presently there appeared an old fellow who, in his black *soutane* and venerable beard, looked as if he had stepped out of that picture of Elijah feeding the ravens.

In Arabic he politely welcomed us to his house and all that was his, in the customary manner; but it didn't take half an eye to see that he was mighty scared, for he well knew that did the Arabs learn that he had sheltered us they would make it a good excuse to sack his home, at the very least.

Yet in spite of that he did not forget his courtesy, and while talking oriental commonplaces caused his daughters to wait on us with wine and sweetmeats on golden plates—young girls with blue-black hair and what I thought big pop eyes. However, Billy seemed to get along with them fine, and evidently they were unanimous in their opinion of him.

Later when Billy explained exactly what we needed I think the old boy was tickled to death that the demand was so light. Anyway he sent a slave out in an almighty hurry to buy *jelabah* of camel hair, a grayish color with bits of colored ribbon scattered about it, and dirty *rozzah*, such as is affected by the country and desert tribes.

We hadn't any means of paying for them, but to offer would not have been etiquette, and I, who had never had much to do with the Jewish element, made a ghastly error by calling down the blessings of Allah upon his venerable head. However, he didn't take it amiss—being accustomed, I guess, to more serious insults than that—and made haste to offer us food.

But he was obviously yearning for our departure; yet he was quite a sport, was old Ibrahim ibn Yusuf, and never by the flicker of an eye did he show how mad he was. He left us alone for an hour after the meal to rest and then came to bid us farewell. Billy didn't see any more of the girls or he might have been tempted to linger. So about eight-thirty A.M. with our rifles slung under our armpits beneath the voluminous *jelabah* we went out into the glare again.

Of course neither Billy nor I knew the road nor, except vaguely, the direction of the palace. We sauntered along in that general direction until we came to the walls of the *millah*, and by following them came to the gate and so into the main city. Wandering through an arch, we found ourselves in the courtyard of a mosque.

In the center, as usual, was the pool for making the ablutions. Now as I hadn't had a bath or even a wash for so long that I couldn't remember the last time, so to speak, that cool water had some attraction. Of course I, during those awful years, had learned every action of the ceremonial ritual; but the trouble was that I didn't know whether Billy did; and as there were two men busy we mighty betray ourselves if Billy unwittingly made a blunder. I asked him in a low voice in Arabic if he knew and he assented; so, strolling up, we doffed our slippers and began.

One of the two men was a hawk-nosed son of a gun who looked like one of our Tuareg friends. As I was at work, longing to strip and get right in, I noticed that he was staring hard. I glanced at Billy, scared that he was making a mess of things; but I couldn't discover anything noticeably wrong except that his rifle was sticking out beneath his robes, as I suppose mine was, about half a foot. But that wasn't anything abnormal.

Then I noticed that the fellow was staring at me, and particularly at my hands. Then I understood. I had forgotten to slip off a ring. Now to orthodox Mohammedans gold ornaments are forbidden, though that didn't worry these people any; but my ring was obviously of European make.

I whispered to Billy to quit right then. We slowly slipped on our shoes and began to walk off. I saw the fellow out of my eye mumbling away to himself. Then he started to follow. Evidently the fact that we hadn't entered the mosque to pray after ablutions was another suspicious point.

I took a hurried glance around and spotted another gate leading out into what looked like a quiet lane. As we made for it I whispered to Billy to get his rifle loose.

At that moment another man came walking across the courtyard, making for the fountain. Swiftly calculating that he wouldn't be in the line of vision by the time our man reached the arch, I whispered again to Billy.

"Pretend to part under the arch. Wait round the corner and I'll slug him as he comes through. If I miss, you must get him. If he starts something, we're lost."

Accordingly, in the arch we faced about and made a pretense of saying good-by, Arab fashion, and then stopped dead on either side of the wall. Fortunately the lane was empty. A minute later came the shuffling of our inquisitive friend. Then I got him.

He went down without any fuss; and after pulling his unconscious body out of sight in order not to disturb the faithful on their way to prayer, we turned to beat it up the lane as fast as we could. But bearing down upon us was a man who must have seen the whole thing.

We both pulled up and began to walk sedately but with our rifles out. As the fellow came on I saw that he had a red beard, and something about him seemed familiar. When he came abreast, but on the other side of the lane, and the sun was straight in our eyes, I nearly let out a yell. However, although he looked us straight in the eyes he didn't seem to know us or to have witnessed what he must have seen. I hesitated. Yet I was dead sure of that puggy nose. Said Billy—

"Wasn't that Vèron?"

We both turned and stared after him. I daren't call out in case it might not be. The fellow kept steadily on.

"Mighty queer," commented Billy. "I could have sworn it was Vèron, and yet— And anyway he must have seen—"

"Me too," said I. "Let's go after and see. Here, I'll tackle him."

But as I started after him three men came in sight. We slowed up and walked sedately along until they were past, but by that time the man whom we suspected had passed into a main street. We followed on doggedly, not daring to hurry after him; and he, we noticed, seemed to have put on the pace a bit.

The street got more and more crowded as we came into a market square beginning to fill with country people and camels, mules and donkeys, and we had some difficulty in keeping the tag on our man. Several times we lost him, only to find him by the glint of that red beard.

Once we nearly got into trouble with a beggar who was holding up people for alms; under the guise of being crazy, and therefore holy; and we unfortunately hadn't any *fluss*—the base Moroccan copper or the cowrie shells, the local change—upon us. However, Billy, with presence of mind, misquoted a *sura* of the Koran, which impressed him enough to give us a chance to slip by and let him focus his attention on the next victim.

After that we had to take a chance and hurry to overtake our man, who had again disappeared. This time we couldn't locate him for some time until we made a sudden turn, when we found ourselves in a large square before what was evidently the palace of the Gandhi, beneath the great arch of which I caught the gleam of his red beard as he stood talking to one of the guards. This time the sun was not in my eyes, but directly upon him, and as he spoke a gesture he made with one hand convinced me.

"By ——, it *is* Vèron!" I exclaimed to Billy, recklessly in English.

But at that moment Red-Beard turned and walked into the palace.

XX

"NOW THAT'S DARNED FUNNY," said Billy in a low tone as, the middle of the square being empty, we turned off. "How did that son-of-a-gun get loose?"

"Same as us, I guess," I retorted. "He can talk like a native, and he passed as one for years."

"But what's he up to anyway? I mean in there?"

"Search me," said I. "How should I know? But he must have recognized us. Why did he refuse to speak?"

"The point is, where are the others? You never know. He may be working to get 'em loose, top. He may not have known us in this Berber get-up. He may—"

"*Skut!*" (Shut up) I whispered as a party of Arabs came toward us, and added in Arabic, "Let us go to the crowd yonder."

We strolled slowly over and into a market being held on the far side of the square. As we wandered silently through the crowd we saw several negroes standing upon blocks evidently slaves for sale.

As I ran my eyes along them I jerked Billy's sleeve to come away, for I had recognized two of our personal servants standing chained and looking very miserable. But I feared that should they see us they might give away our identity by some appeal for help.

Farther along was another crowd. We approached it cautiously, attracted by some one volubly holding forth like a soapbox politician. As we came nearer I pricked up my ears at the repeated mention of "infidel" and "doctor." We lingered on the outskirts and listened.

The man was Doc Seeger's boy. We pushed and elbowed our way closer; and then I got a shock, for, squatting on the ground, was the doc himself. I nudged Billy, thinking—

"Darnation, the whole gang seems to have broken loose; but we—well, we were loose, too, in a way, but we have lost Fieldmorre."

Billy had seen, and we edged still closer until we were in the second rank of the crowd. The doc's boy was holding forth about the generosity of the Sultan Gandhi, who had taken under his protection the infidel doctor, who had, according to the law, been pardoned for his ignorance, as he had consented to become a Mohammedan—

Under all this bunk—which I guessed right away meant that the Gandhi was going to try to kid the doctor into being his own medical advisor, instead of trusting to mixtures of medieval surgery and magic—the doc, whose knowledge of Arabic was of the slightest, sat grinning amiably without a notion of what was being said.

Unable to speak, Billy and I concentrated our gaze on him, trying to catch his eye, but it was some time before he would cease smirking in every direction except ours. At last he did, and I saw the idiot start in surprise. But a finger on my lips kept him quiet until he had time to think things out.

Almost imperceptibly I gestured to get away somehow, and he got it. He seemed pretty free, for immediately he rose, and in broken Arabic told his man he wanted to go home.

The boy, being fond of his own voice and the attention his charge was exciting, continued yapping for a while; but when the doc grew insistent, obeyed, clearing a way, with many insulting jests at the unconscious "convert," through the crowd. We followed, of course, and also the usual crowd.

He made for a small gate in the palace wall not far away, giving us a look as he went in. We dawdled about, but to our disgust so did several of the overcurious, just the same way as our own folk will stare till their eyeballs ache at the house where the latest murder has been committed.

As we waited, suddenly the drums and wailing pipes broke out quite near us.

"We'd better get a taxi," whispered Billy, "or we won't get a seat."

About twenty minutes later I saw that the small wicket window in the gate was opened slightly. Evidently the doc was peeking out to see if we were there and the road was clear. At last, although there were still half a dozen idiots loafing about, I whispered to Billy—

"Let's lounge against the door as if we were born tired, and maybe if the doc's there he'll let us slip in."

By degrees, we edged over and squatted down on the threshold. Presently we heard the breathing of some one on the other side and the creak of the window door, and the doc's voice said:

"Oh, my ——, is that really you chaps?"

"Sure," I replied. "Can't you let us in?"

We heard a bolt creak and he whispered—

"Quick!"

We rose and slipped inside. We were in a garden thickly screened with trees and shrubs.

"By ——, I am glad to see you!" exclaimed Doc Seeger, and he looked it. "But, *ssh!* Don't talk too loud. Come here; I daren't take you in the house."

He led the way into the shrubbery, and we crouched under a bush.

"Where's that enterprising nigger of yours?" demanded Billy.

"I don't quite trust him," said the doc. "But he loves the needle, so I gave him a shot of morphia to keep him quiet."

"But," said I, "where are the others? Hardwicke and the men? Have you seen Vèron?"

"Haven't seen Vèron nor Hardwicke, but I was kept with the other fellows until we arrived here. Then they brought me to the sultan. Seems rather a decent sort. He assured me that you fellows were all right and that if I'd treat him he'd make us all rich. He's suffering from scorbutic troubles. Gave me this house here and my own boy, but he's got too darned cheeky.

"But, man, the country's lousy with gold! Where have you got your place?"

"Our what?" queried Billy.

"Your house. He told me that you were his guests and that he had put you up in another wing of the palace."

"Didn't you think it kind of queer," said I, "that you were never allowed to see us?"

"Yes, I did, but he spun a long yarn about trouble with his fanatical people and said that for a week it was better to keep us apart. But where's Lord Fieldmorre?"

We told him briefly what had happened. He whistled softly.

"My ——, if I'd known that, I'd have given him a shot that would have kept him quiet, the swine!"

"That wouldn't have been any darn good," retorted Billy, "for there's another crazy guy," and he told him about Sabah.

"Well, I'm ——!" exploded Seeger. "I shouldn't have suspected him. Thought he was absolutely devoted to Lord Fieldmorre. Everybody seems going off their heads. But what about Vèron?"

We related the little we knew about him, and he couldn't throw any light on the problem. He didn't even know where the other men were located, for he had been led to the Gandhi at night and had straightway been taken to his new quarters in the palace.

"I thought the whole thing ruddy funny," he remarked. "But he seemed a decent sort and I thought the best thing I could do was to submit and see what was going to happen."

"Sure," I assented. "Wouldn't have got you anywhere if you had kicked. Anyway he wouldn't have crucified you—at least not until he caught another white doctor. Got any guns?"

"Yes," said he. "That's funny, too. They took away all the other fellows' arms but let me keep my Mauser pistol. In fact, I felt rather rotten because they made a fuss of me all along the road—as a doctor, you know."

"Sure," said Billy; "that was that swine Sabah's doing. There's a big show tonight," he continued, and told the doc our suspicions. "And, see here, guess you'd better get that gun and come along with us unless you'd rather stop here. You're free to do as you like, doc, for the expedition's busted all right."

"Of course I'll come along with you, you chaps—unless you think I'd do better by sticking a needle into that Levantine rat."

"Too late," said Billy. "But, look here, Seeger, we want you to understand that you've got a chance to save yourself. Ours is pretty rocky as far as we can see. But we feel it's up to us to try to help Fieldmorre and the boys from a filthy death, although the chances are that we all go under together. That's about all there is to it.

"What Vèron's up to I can't get. Of course he may be working or trying to work with us once he gets in touch. He may be in touch with the boys and maybe he ain't. Anyway that's about all there is to it. Isn't that right, Phil?"

"Sure," said I.

"Good ——!" exclaimed the doc. "There isn't any question. You fellows don't think a white man's going to sit here and see you chaps hacked to pieces without inquiring why? I'll get my pistol now. And— But what exactly is the plan?"

I described for his benefit the snake outfit and the pleasant things the

Gandhi had promised to do with us, which evidently he had every intention of carrying out.

"There is a faint chance," I added, "that Sabah may somehow pry this other guy out of the sultan job and do something for us; but personally I reckon I wouldn't waste a dime on the betting. We aim to get in with the bunch and find out whether they really are set on carrying out the crucifying stunt. If that's so, all we can do is to save them from torture by shooting them ourselves and then—good night, nursie! Get me?"

Doc Seeger gazed at me searchingly.

"You really think it's as bad as that, Tromp?"

"Sure I do! I know 'em. Don't forget that!"

"That's true."

He rose.

"All right," he added. "I won't be a sec."

"Say," said Billy, "if you can, you'd best get another robe from some one. Like ours if you can."

"All right; I'll borrow my boy's. He'll sleep peacefully for an hour or more. I say, d'you want anything to eat before we start?"

But neither Billy nor I felt any need. Within a few minutes he returned in the rough *jelab* of his servant. I looked him over. Fortunately, Seeger was dark and his beard was fairly long and ragged—in fact he would pass muster better than Billy or I, although fair Berbers were common enough, to which fact we owed the safety of our disguise.

"Anyway pull your hood well over your face," was all I could suggest to shadow the unusual blueness of his eyes.

At the garden gate we took the precaution to peek through the latchet window, but most of the loafers had gone. Across the square were many people streaming in one direction.

"Early doors, two bits," commented Billy flippantly as we went through.

Cautioning the doc to keep his mouth shut in any circumstances, we followed on and joined the throng on foot, composed of the usual Mandingo population, mixed negro-Berber with a sprinkling of lower-class women muffled to the eyes in the *haik* or blanket.

We had again slung our guns under our armpits and beneath the *jelabah*, envying the portability of the doc's Mauser and wooden stock-case. In the general hum of conversation about I caught a few words from a group of higher-class Berbers who were gravely discussing some prophecy made by an *imam* in a certain mosque frequented by the sect of the Druse, to the effect that there would appear at this sacred festival the reincarnation of Darazi the prophet—evidently, I reckoned, some of Sabah's propaganda.

Other words picked up here and there regarding "infidels" and the "lords of the forest" gave me an inkling that the Gandhi intended to carry out the fiendish atrocities he had promised, apparently upon the boys whom he still had in captivity.

I've faced the final proposition several times before, but just the same a fellow doesn't get used to it—at least I don't. I've got lots of red blood and can see ahead lots of fun in life. I was fond of Billy and other people I had known and knew and hoped to meet again. But those words meant, if they meant anything, that the end wasn't very far off; for, as we had agreed, there was only one thing to do and only one way out.

I swore under my breath in good American at the luck of it, the treachery of Sabah and the bobbing-up, of all people in the world, of this little Levantine whose face I'd smacked for woman-beating. Yet there was a faint chance that Sabah might redeem himself, which Billy seemed to think possible, but I didn't.

A crook may play straight with his kind, but a traitor never will; at any rate not a fanatical Islamite against Christians. However, I'd got a nearly full bandoleer and a gun, which was considerably better than to be strung up like a chicken to have my neck wrung.

While I was indulging in these cheerful ideas Billy tugged at my sleeve, motioning me to slow down. I followed his glance ahead, and after a bit spotted on the right five of our late Hausa soldiers. If they recognized us the row would start right there, and that was the last thing we wanted.

I pulled my hood farther over my face, and we dropped back into the crowd, edging toward the other side. While I was calculating the chances of the others being about or near us in the arena Billy got the right idea.

Nudging me, he unrolled the first band of his *rozzah* and wrapped it across his face mask fashion, leaving only the eyes exposed. That we should do so meant little in this country. A Tuareg would always wear his veil, which was really used to keep out the desert sand, even in a town; and anyway bandits and other gentry who don't wish to be recognized adopt the same method without raising comment on a fete day.

Scarcely had we done so than right under my nose appeared the very Hausa who had knocked me out from behind when I was foolishly staring at the giant monitor. I sure did long to reach out and get a grip of that man, but it couldn't be done.

The drums were still going. Presently we swung with the crowd to the right. At the bottom of the great square were two big, arched gates evidently leading into the temple, which was, I knew, attached to the palace. Outside the crowd surged and swayed and chattered just like a bunch waiting to get into Madison Square Garden. It was too risky to talk, in case some one spotted our accent, but to keep up appearances I fumbled beneath my *jelab* as if I were telling my beads and mumbled incessantly—

"Allah-lah, lah-Allah!"

Billy, tumbling to the idea, followed suit, so no doubt as extra holy guys we attracted little attention.

We drifted with the tide to the northern gate. Fortunately, in the east they're not great on tickets, particularly for a sacred stunt such as this was, so that except for the guards lounging about the gate of the entrance there was no one to challenge us. As we approached, the crowd of course became denser and denser until we were packed as tight as sardines in a can and, whew! How they stank!

At length, without mishap, we got through the zigzag gate and into the temple, which of course I had seen before with the Gandhi. All the steps running up to the buildings walling in three sides were white with humanity, and the roofs were packed with women looking with dark faces sticking out of their *haiks* like penguins on an iceberg. Driven in the rush, as we entered we found ourselves to the left. Thinking of possible eventualities, I risked something by whispering into Billy's ear in Arabic—

"Up against the wall!"

By furious elbow and shoulder work, and guttural grunts by way of retaliatory oaths, we gained at last not the wall, but pretty near and beneath the arched portico.

The swimming-pool was empty, and the waters of the lake, ending in the sacred grove where we had hidden, glittered in the brilliant sun. The ivory-and-gold throne of the Gandhi, directly beneath us and about fifty yards' rifle-shot away, was empty, and about it was a large space.

Behind this kind of stage was another dais filled with men in white robes and green turbans. The drums and wailing of the pipes came from somewhere hidden behind.

Evidently we had just got in in time, for above the hum of general talk came outcries as the guards were closing out the rest. The stream of people ceased, and the rhythm of the drums suddenly increased and stopped abruptly.

An *imam* standing by a large gate in the palace building side began to cry out in the wailing voice of the *muezzin*, and the crowd became silent. The door opened, and the Gandhi appeared—in white from head to foot, as I had seen him, with the great emerald glittering on his turban. About him was a bunch of some two dozen of the gorgeously dressed nobles.

As he walked in silence to the throne all bent low their heads, and we had to follow suit. When he was seated the noble fellows squatted down between him and the priests.

There was silence for a few moments, and I wondered what was going to happen. Then I spotted a commotion in the same door from which the Gandhi had emerged, and amid a rushing sound of approval and satisfaction there appeared a party of eunuchs carrying, bound to a cross, the naked form of Fieldmorre. I recognized him instantly by the blob of the bleeding wound on his thigh.

"My ——!" I exclaimed, half-starting to my feet.

"Shut up, you fool!" whispered Billy, grabbing my wrist. "Wait!"

Fortunately our neighbors were too absorbed in this pleasant spectacle to notice my diversion.

After Fieldmorre were borne Pexton, Hibbert and O'Donnell; and the four were staked in ready-made holes on the edge of the water.

XXI

I SET MY TEETH AND REMAINED QUIET, working my rifle loose as I watched. From the distance I couldn't see for sure whether they were in pain or not, but none gave a cry or even cursed. A guttural oath of satisfaction that "the lords of the forest" would be well entertained by so goodly a number of infidels nigh broke my resolve to keep my tongue still. And from all sides came guttural murmurs of approval, faintly echoed in the lighter tones and squeals from the women on the roofs.

Then suddenly there rose the thin wail of the Gandhi reed pipe. Against the white of his robes I could see the black head of the cobra appear, glide from the throat-slit of the *silham* and coil around and up until as before the snake's head was swaying above the emerald on the turban. At that everybody became silent, only the tight breathing registering the excitement of nervous expectancy.

A guttural grunt near me brought my eyes out to the lake and I nudged Billy's arm. On the glittering surface of the sunlit water appeared a ripple and two moving specks, leaving in their wakes molten silver streaks. A quivering "u-h-h!" ran through the crowd, and every man craned forward, staring fixedly at the advancing serpents. Other dots of silver wreaths appeared behind.

The wailing pipe continued rising and falling in that creepy way it had. In the water of the tank, the pythons glinted in the sun. The leader seemed to hurl or shoot itself beyond the stone lip on to the earth; but the second reared, and, failing to get a grip with its flexible ribs, slid back into the water and disappeared. Another glided over seemingly without effort.

One after another they came, obeying the strange call, passing close beneath the crosses bearing the victims, until there were some thirteen or fourteen serpents arranged around the white-shrouded figure on the gold-and-ivory throne, their chromatic bodies swaying to the crying of the pipe, the hideous cobra on the head of Gandhi seeming to beat time like some ghastly conductor.

What was going to happen next I did not know, since the Gandhi had merely given me a kind of exhibition show, I guessed, by way of something for me to think about. I could see Pexton and O'Donnell twisting their heads sidewise to peer down in an effort to see what was going on beneath them. Fieldmorre either was unconscious of them or resigned, but I could see the strain of his shoulder muscles as he tried to take the weight off his wounded leg.

Then just as I was wondering how long this performance was going on and what was to happen, I started as I heard from a little to the right among a group of robed figures the preliminary squeak of another pipe. As the thin wail trickled out hundreds of heads turned in that direction, and I sighed with a feeling of relief, thinking that this was Sabah starting in to redeem his promise.

At first I couldn't make out what he was after. The sound rose in volume, and in some way I couldn't define, the rhythm or tune was slightly different from that of the Gandhi, who had flashed an angry glance in the direction of the interloper, but was still playing. Then, accompanied by a half-suppressed "uh" of astonishment from the crowd, I saw two pythons sway away from the charmer on the throne and begin to glide toward the rival.

One after another the others followed the lead. The Gandhi's pipe rose in volume and speed; but even the black cobra coiled down his shoulders and across the floor to the new music, which seemed irresistible, and climbed up on Sabah's head.

As the first two serpents approached Sabah those about him scattered in violent haste until there was a space as big as that around the throne about him. Within ten minutes every serpent had deserted the Gandhi and was swaying ecstatically around the squatted form of Sabah!

Suddenly the Gandhi ceased playing, and, leaping to his feet, shouted angrily to his gorgeous body-guard to seize the sacrilegious stranger. Some of them started forward, some raised their guns, but more hung back.

I saw Sabah's clever move. None of them dared attack while the holy snakes were about him. The Gandhi lost his cold dignity and shouted and cursed futilely, recalling the time I had stopped him beating up the woman slave.

Among the green-turbaned priests at the back an excited discussion was going on, but the great audience seemed too astonished or awed to do much beyond stare and gasp oaths upon Allah to the accompaniment of subdued squeaks and cries from the roofs.

The Gandhi, shrieking with rage, turned upon his nobles, who, clustering around him, fell to shouting and protesting; and above the din the wail of Sabah's pipe played on and on, and the pythons swayed their chromatic bodies as if they were being driven crazy with excitement by the cobra conductor on Sabah's head.

Evidently, thought I, there was no precedent for such a happening, so that none of them knew what ought to be done. As I was wondering whether Sabah intended to try to wear out the dancing snakes until they were harmless from fatigue or whether he was waiting for some expected reinforcements to arrive, there came a gasp from the crowd, bringing my eyes back in time to see him take the pipe from his mouth and stick it within his *jelab*, where, with his fingers still operating the holes, it continued to play as loudly as ever.

He had me puzzled, and for a moment I almost thought—noticing a gentle undulation going on beneath his robe—what the natives had evidently thought; that a snake was actually blowing into the instrument. Then of course I tumbled. He'd got a bagpipe arrangement concealed beneath his *jelab*.

Then in a high, piercing voice that was audible all over the place he began to talk, a long-winded affair, claiming that he was a kind of messiah and the next incarnation of the Druse prophet, Darazi, mixed up with a lot of muddled Mohammedan law, and the crazy yarn of his descent from Abgar Ukkama and all the rest of it.

No sooner had he paused for a moment than a band near to him, who were evidently his pals, began to shriek—

"Messiah!"

With the pipe still wailing, but more softly, and the pythons working like a Broadway ballet, he began again making some sort of challenge to the group of holy men, or *ullema* as he called them, in the green turbans, finishing up with a regular Tammany attack upon the Gandhi, calling him names that an Egyptian donkey boy would surely admire.

He had some powers of oratory, had Sabah, when he fairly got going; for he held that bunch against what the Gandhi and what was left of his partisans could do to drown him, and finished by having the whole crowd on its feet yelling for the Gandhi's gore. Then, evidently reckoning that he was safe from the mob, he ceased playing. As soon as the pythons began to glide back to the water the row subsided a bit, and all eyes watched them as if expecting them to make some signal or to read the supposed meaning of their movements.

Even the cobra snuggled into his clothes, as much at home as with its late master. Anyway it seemed all right for him, for he rose and walked sedately in their wake. The Gandhi, who appeared to have lost his head entirely or had realized that the game was up, stood silent with one hand on the throne.

Then, halting abruptly, Sabah raised one hand up, called out some phrase in a chanting voice which I didn't catch, probably in Aramaic, which seemed to be his trump card, for instantly came a roar of assent. Then, pointing to the Gandhi, he commanded the gang of nobles, who were standing in a bunch like a flock of scared sheep, to throw their sultan to the lords of the forest.

Immediately three of them walked out gravely and took hold of the Gandhi, who, to my astonishment, didn't appear to attempt to struggle, nor did he cry out as, picking him up, they walked deliberately to the water edge and threw him in.

The splash sounded in dead silence. He disappeared, came up, and began to swim. Then suddenly a hand shot up, and his screech echoed against the palace walls. There was a glint of colors amid the swash of a chromatic body in a swirl, and he had disappeared. For all that his fate was our salvation, I couldn't help but shudder.

As soon as the ripples had subsided Sabah turned, walking very slowly, watched by all, and took his seat on the empty throne.

"By ——, he's got away with it," I muttered to Billy; fortunately I wasn't remarked by my absorbed neighbors.

"Now," thought I with a mighty feeling of relief, "I guess he'll get busy and cut down Fieldmorre and the rest."

As soon as he was seated he drew out the pipe again and began to play as before. Out came the cobra and climbed around his head, and from the water returned the pythons.

"What the ——," I muttered angrily to myself, "is he after now?"

And I tried to comfort my anxiety with the thought that he was playing safe to fool the crowd and get 'em tame or something.

When the brutes were about him in full blast of their hideous dance he again switched on the bagpipe gear and began to chant something—in Aramaic, I suppose—which I didn't understand.

My toes were twitching in nervous impatience when a movement to one side caught my attention. From behind the group of nobles and priests at the back of the throne came running some men got up in the same colored robes as the man Billy had shot in the night whom we'd found dead in the old temple. They came down at a trot to the four crosses, and as the thought was halfway into my mind that they were going to release our pals the foremost lifted a kind of staff and smashed O'Donnell across the shins, breaking his leg.

The word "Ahab" flashed into my mind, and I yelled to Billy and the doc: "It's all up! Get those swine first!"

I dragged out my rifle and fired at Sabah. As Billy's rifle and the doc's Mauser spoke Sabah slumped across the throne, and two of the executioners dropped in their tracks.

XXII

As I JERKED ANOTHER CARTRIDGE INTO PLACE, hoping that we should have time to rescue the four from Ahab's death by torture, there broke out a sudden familiar rattle followed by shrieks. In a glance I saw that it came from the roof over the sultan's palace.

Against a background of flying women I got a glimpse of a red beard.

"Vèron!" I yelled. "Fight our way down and make for the palace!"

But Billy and the doc had caught on as quickly as I. Fortunately our neighbors were either unarmed or too dumfounded to attack. Swinging our guns right and left, we had comparatively little trouble in smashing a path through the shouting, swearing crowd.

But in the open space was a sight which made me, even in that moment, draw back; for Vèron had turned his first volley right upon the mass of dancing snakes, and now they were fleeing for the water, those that were left, while the others squirmed and writhed in chromatic knots.

Billy, who had no childish fears, dashed among them toward the four crucified. I followed, observing that the machine gun was deliberately playing over our heads, spraying in a deadly half-circle to keep them off us, taking no notice whatever of the frantic crowd tramping each other to get through the gates.

In a nightmare of writhing pythons about us I made for Fieldmorre, and, not stopping to try to cut or untie his bonds, picked him and the cross up bodily. As I did so I caught a signal from Vèron on the roof to make for the palace. Whether it was the doc or Billy who cut the other three loose or not I never knew; but as I staggered with my burden I was conscious of Billy, bearing O'Donnell with the smashed shin, and the other two passing me.

We reached the gates and some one slammed it behind us. Then the Maxim stopped.

My first action naturally was to see to my rescue, Fieldmorre, who, as the doc hacked at his bonds, smiled grimly and whispered—

"Thanks awfully, Tromp."

He was in a pretty bad mess, but insisted upon borrowing a robe to cover himself. As the doc got busy making temporary splints for O'Donnell the red beard of Vèron appeared in the large room, shouting excitedly in French.

"Come on, you fellows!" exclaimed Fieldmorre, limping toward the stairway. "Vèron says we'll have to stand off an attack."

Grabbing my gun, which somehow I'd had the sense not to let go of, I followed him to the roof together with Billy, Hibbert and Pexton. All the women had naturally quit *pronto*. While Vèron jabbered rapidly to Fieldmorre, I took a look around.

In the temple of snakes there was nobody left at all except the scattered corpses of those shot. To my surprize the open market square was empty too, but from the row going on just around the corner I guessed that they were pulling themselves together for the final rush.

In that pause it suddenly occurred to me that although Vèron had rescued us it wouldn't help any after all, except that we would be able to make 'em pay the more dearly.

As far as I knew we had neither food nor water; and even if we could manage to grab water from the pool beneath and find food somewhere, sooner or later they'd get us through sheer weight of numbers as they had Gordon in Khartum. I had just fired at the hint of a turban peeking around a corner of the street and was trying to figure out how long they'd take to reorganize enough to rush, when Billy and Pexton joined me.

"Say, Phil," Billy remarked, "don't you think it's darned queer they don't make a rush to finish us? What's to stop 'em anyway?"

"Indeed that's what I was saying," added Pexton.

Just then we all three started at the unmistakable angry rattle of *mitrailleuses*. The sounds came from several directions at once and were accompanied by erratic volleys from rifles. As we stared wonderingly we noticed a parcel of natives dash excitedly across the deserted square as if they had forgotten we were on the roof.

"Good ——!" exclaimed Billy. "Sounds like a relief column! But that's impossible!"

"Perhaps," suggested Pexton, "they've started scrapping among themselves—Sabah's part, I mean, against the others."

"Glory," I was beginning, "if that's so, maybe we'll have a chance. Let's get—"

But at that moment Fieldmorre hailed us from where he was seated on the coping of the roof talking to Vèron. He said quietly as if apologizing formally for bumping against a fellow coming out of a show:

"William, and you, Tromp, I'm afraid that I owe you an apology all round." I stared dumbly, thinking maybe he was a bit delirious. There was a queer, tight look about his mouth which wasn't on account of pain or exhaustion; something seemed to have angered him into almost forgetting his suffering.

"It seems that we've been betrayed all along. D'you hear those guns there? That's a French column."

"French column!" I echoed stupidly.

"What—Vèron—" began Billy, seizing upon the truth more quickly than I.

"Yes; you're right, William. As a matter of fact I suppose it doesn't much matter, for if it hadn't been for his—er—patriotism, if you like, we should have been most certainly wiped out. Isn't that so?

"You see it's like this," he continued, wearily holding his forehead. "The Captain Vèron is in the French service, as you knew, the significance of which we, William, possibly failed to recognize down below there. He, it seemed, somewhat mistook our characters and endeavored, he tells me, to frighten us away from exploring in this direction."

He smiled contemptuously.

"Then when he realized that we—er—reacted in a different manner he was compelled to report the circumstances to the French authorities, who ordered him to remain with us as—er—secret-service agent, you understand, at the same time dispatching a powerful column in order to secure the territory for France."

Neither Billy nor I said anything, but looked at Vèron, who was standing some few feet away staring across the town toward the sound of the firing, which had increased in volume, through his Zeiss glasses.

"I quite see his point of view. Had we been successful, as you know, the country would have become nominally British. These international jealousies—I'm afraid the rest is somewhat obvious."

We three remained silent.

"Hardwicke was right!" exclaimed Billy. "What has happened to him?"

"Killed, as far as Vèron could find out, by those *sumpitan* people."

"And Thorpe?" said I.

"Sacrificed a long while ago as we were to have been today."

"Why the —— did Vèron desert us at the first village?" demanded Billy with a touch of anger.

"Orders, so I understand, to foment discord in order to attract attention from the French advance from the Sudan—the east, you know. He it was, apparently, who assisted the amiable Sabah to secure converts. Very able man undoubtedly. Oh, by the way, I understand that he is empowered to offer us some consideration—concessions of some sort. How d'you fellows feel, what?"

"Nothing doing for me," said I sharply. "I guess we owe him our lives maybe, but nothing else if I know it."

"That's right," agreed Billy promptly. "After this I'll retire, for only national pirates can get away with it these days."

THE END

OFF-TRAIL PUBLICATIONS

Specializing in the era of American pulp fiction

THE WEIRD DETECTIVE ADVENTURES OF WADE HAMMOND

By Paul Chadwick

Volume 1: 10 stories, 180 pages, $18
Volume 2: 10 stories, 172 pages, $18
Volume 3: 10 stories, 202 pages, $18
Volume 4: 9 stories, 232 pages, $18

The Wade Hammond stories complete in four volumes. In these chilling adventures, all from the classic 1930's pulps, Detective-Dragnet *and* Ten Detective Aces, *freelance investigator Wade Hammond battles a series of weird enemies. Some of the best of '30s pulp fiction.*

DOCTOR COFFIN: The Living Dead Man

By Perley Poore Sheehan • Introduction by John Wooley

8 novelettes, 178 pages, $16

Weird stories from Thrilling Detective, *1932-33. A former character actor who faked his own death, Doctor Coffin runs a string of mortuaries by night and fights crime at night. One of the strangest detective series.*

SUPER-DETECTIVE FLIP BOOK: Two Complete Novels

From the pulp *Super-Detective*:

"Legion of Robots" (November 1940) by Victor Rousseau • Introduction by John McMahan •• "Murder's Migrants" (March 1943) by Robert Leslie Bellem and W.T. Ballard • Introduction by John Wooley

2 short novels, 174 pages, $18

Super-Detective started as a Doc Savage-like adventure pulp, then changed format to hardboiled detective. The Flip Book *features a novel from each of the two phases with intros exploring the historical background. Exciting!*

AMAZON STORIES
Volume 1: Pedro & Lourenço
Volume 2: Pedro & Lourenço
By Arthur O. Friel • Introductions by John Locke
Vol 1: 10 stories, 222 pages, $18 • **Vol 2**: 10 stories, 286 pages, $20

Collects Friel's first twenty stories from Adventure *(1919-21), following the strange experiences of two Amazon Basin rubber workers as they explore the jungle. The best of pulp adventure fiction.*

GROTTOS OF CHINATOWN: The Dorus Noel Stories
By Arthur J. Burks • Introduction by John Locke
11 stories, 194 pages, $16

The complete adventures of Dorus Noel from All Detective Magazine *(1933-34). Burks' Manhattan Chinatown is a place of dark mystery, riddled with secret passageways, menaced by hatchetmen. Introduction discusses the history of* All Detective *and the career of the Speed-King of the Pulps, Arthur J. Burks.*

THE GOLDEN ANACONDA: And Other Strange Tales of Adventure
By Elmer Brown Mason • Introduction by John Locke
10 stories, 260 pages, $20

Fantastic and horror-laden stories set in the exotic corners of the world known to their globe-trotting entomologist author. Includes all five Wandering Smith stories from The Popular Magazine; *and five tales from* All-Story Weekly. *All published, 1915-16.*

CITY OF NUMBERED MEN: The Best of Prison Stories
Introduction by John Locke
12 stories, 278 pages, $20

During Prohibition, famed publisher Harold Hersey turned America's disintegrating prison system into the hardboiled Prison Stories *(1930-31). Included are stories from all issues of this rare pulp, the startling history of* Prison Stories, *cover gallery, and the first comprehensive biography of pulp publishing's most colorful character, Harold Hersey.*

THE MAGICIAN DETECTIVE: And Other Weird Mysteries
By Fulton Oursler
Introduction by John Locke
7 stories, 210 pages, $18

Fulton Oursler was one of the great editors of his time, ruling over the Macfadden publishing empire for two decades. But stage magic was his first love. In this collection of early fiction, Oursler's bewitching imagination takes flight in tales of magic, murder and mystery. Featured is an exploration of the astonishing career of Fulton Oursler.

GHOST STORIES: The Magazine and Its Makers
Edited by John Locke
Vol 1: 19 stories, 256 pages, $24 • **Vol 2**: 15 stories, 272 pages, $24

Macfadden's Ghost Stories *(1926-31) presented haunted tales in every exciting arena: the Western Front, gangland, aviation, the Klondike, the circus, etc. The personnel behind* Ghost Stories *were a fascinating group: poets and scholars, war heroes and war correspondents, adventurers and Bohemians; a few became prolific pulpsters; a few became bestselling authors. And a few led haunted lives. Vol 1 includes the history of* Ghost Stories, *bios of every editor, and every Vol 1 author. Vol 2 includes bios of every Vol 2 author, every cover artist, and a gallery of all 64* Ghost Stories *covers.*

HOBO STORIES
By Patrick & Terence Casey • Introduction by John Locke
6 stories, 332 pages, $20

The Caseys were two brothers from San Francisco who broke into the pulps while still teenagers. Within a few years, they had conned their way into the prestigious pages of Adventure. Hobo Stories *reprints their series of exploits of a teenage hobo and his dog from* The Saturday Evening Post *(1914) and* Adventure *(1916-21). Included is their story of a teenage pulp writer from* Romance *(1920); and a lengthy introduction which explores the lives of the Caseys and the origins of their hobo stories.*

OUTDOOR STORIES
By J. Allan Dunn • Introduction by John Locke
3 stories, 190 pages, $16

> *Presented are all three of Dunn's tales from the ultra-rare* Outdoor
> Stories *(1927-28). These gripping adventures, set in the exotic plac-
> es of another day, rank with Dunn's best. The featured story, "New
> Guinea Gold," is an epic tale of friendship, survival and revenge. In-
> cluded is a history of* Outdoor Stories, *a biography of editor Edmund
> C. Richards, and an examination of Dunn's role in the magazine.*

THE PERIL OF THE PACIFIC: The Complete PEOPLE's Serial
By J. Allan Dunn • Introduction by John Locke
168 pages, $14

> *Dunn's Japanese invasion epic is future history, published as a five-
> part serial in* People's *in 1916, but set in 1920.* Peril *pits a force
> of American irregulars armed with futuristic technology against a
> relentless naval empire bent on conquest. Dunn uses San Francisco
> and California's Central Coast as his main settings, drawing upon his
> well-traveled past more than in any other story he ever published.*

IF SHE ONLY HAD A MACHINE GUN: Crime Stories by Richard Credicott
Introductions by Dave Credicott & John Locke
Edited by John Locke & Rob Preston
18 stories, 360 pages, $20

> *The complete stories of one of the best gang-pulp authors. Includes
> gang stories from* Racketeer Stories, Mobs, *etc., wildly entertaining
> tales of mob intrigue and mayhem, and the violent whims of molls;
> and detective stories from* The Dragnet, Dime Detective, *and others.
> All from 1929-33. A complete biographical profile offers rare insights
> into the pulps during the early years of the Depression. As a special
> feature, Dave Credicott provides reminiscences of his father's life.*

All books available from Amazon.com, other online booksellers, and dealers
specializing in the pulps..

QUEEN OF THE GANGSTERS: Volume 1: Broadwalk Empire
Introductions by David Bischoff & John Locke
8 stories, 234 pages, $18

Tough, rough, remorseless stories from the first woman hardboiled crime fiction writer; from gang pulps like Gangland Stories, Racketeer Stories *and* Mobs. *Margie Harris slammed her typewriter like a machine gun, mowing down good guys and bad guys alike; shooting them, knifing them, blowing them up—lacing her prose with metaphysical commentary on the destinations of their damned souls. This is the first time her work has been collected. Introduction from bestselling author David Bischoff.*

www.ingramcontent.com/pod-product-compliance
Lightning Source LLC
Chambersburg PA
CBHW051842170626
46807CB00003B/1300

9 781935 031192